"Why couldn't you get married in a church instead of outside?"

Mrs. Marlowe glanced around, shaking her head as she straightened her son's tie. "How you convinced Andrea's parents here to go along with this crazy scheme of yours, I'll never know."

Kurt pulled away from his mother's fussing and took Andrea in his arms. "We *do* have a minister, Mother," he said wryly, his whole attention focused on his bride.

Andrea thrilled to Kurt's touch as his fingers adjusted her veil, tugged astray by the breeze. Her long white gown swirled around her ankles in the gentle wind.

"And we have *this*." Kurt gestured behind him toward the Grand Canyon, which formed the backdrop to their wedding party.

The cloudless sky was a brilliant azure blue. And the sun shone down on the Canyon's rainbow of colors with a special radiance Andrea knew was just for them.

Dear Reader,

Harlequin Romance's Bridal Collection provided a very special opportunity for me, because in many ways, this story parallels my own prewedding romance. My hero and heroine can't seem to agree on *anything,* and for a while it seemed as if my future husband and I couldn't, either! Roger wanted to marry me after *two*—yes, two—dates, while I couldn't even spell his last name. I was trying to discourage my old college flame from proposing, and meanwhile my new suitor was pestering me with annoying regularity! For six hair-pulling weeks, he was forever showing up at my home, my job and my favorite haunts. He even used his car to block mine in the parking lot so I'd have to seek him out.

Needless to say, his proposal was entirely unconventional. My military suitor said, "I have orders to leave. Are you coming with me?" Talk about do or die!

I finally came to my senses and gave him the answer he wanted. It wasn't hearts and flowers, it wasn't candlelight dinners and violins, but whatever it was has lasted fifteen years. To me, the best romances happen when all the conventions are thrown out the window. To my everlasting gratitude, my husband still lives—and loves—by his own rules.

And so do my hero and heroine. They aren't exactly conventional characters either, but I think you'll enjoy Kurt and Andrea's courtship. *Rescued by Love* is their story—and yours!

Sincerely,

Anne Marie Duquette

RESCUED BY LOVE
Anne Marie Duquette

Harlequin Books

TORONTO • NEW YORK • LONDON
AMSTERDAM • PARIS • SYDNEY • HAMBURG
STOCKHOLM • ATHENS • TOKYO • MILAN
MADRID • WARSAW • BUDAPEST • AUCKLAND

ISBN 0-373-03253-6

Harlequin Romance first edition March 1993

RESCUED BY LOVE

CHAPTER ONE

"A STEWARDESS! I CAN'T believe you hired a damn stewardess!"

Andrea Claybourne fumed at the outrage in the man's voice. She adjusted her skirt, crossed her legs, and listened intently to the argument going on behind Personnel Director Jim Stevens's open door. She couldn't see the two occupants, but she could certainly hear them.

"I believe the correct term is flight attendant," was Jim's calm response.

"Call her whatever you want, Jim, but give me a break!" The nameless man made no attempt to lower his voice. "You can't possibly expect me to train a woman who's spent the last five years mixing cocktails, applying makeup and using a can of hair spray a day!"

Andrea's blood boiled at the insult. Despite herself, she raised one hand to check her smooth honey-blond hair as she listened for Jim's response.

"Andrea Claybourne knows more than how to mix a drink," he said. "She went back to school during her airline career. She's a registered Emergency Medical Technician."

"An E.M.T. without experience is no good to the ranger staff," the other man protested. Andrea didn't like the sound of his brusque, dismissive voice. "This is the Grand Canyon, Jim, not some cushy airline hop! During the summer this park gets over forty-thousand visitors a *day!* You *know* how many people end up on medivac flights. We have

six to seven serious injuries every working shift! This
woman won't be able to handle it.''

Andrea thought grimly of the plane crash she'd walked
away from two months ago. *I can handle more than just
cushy hops, mister.*

"Look, Kurt . . ." Jim began in a conciliatory voice.

So, Mister Rude had a name.

". . . I assure you that Andrea Claybourne's qualified for
the job.''

Andrea heard a loud snort, and then papers rustling.

"There's nothing on this application that says so. All I see
are a couple of class clinicals and a short internship at Fitz-
simmons Army Hospital. It's bad enough that she has no
ranger background, let alone no E.M.T. experience!''

Wrong again, mister, Andrea silently corrected. *I have
experience, and I earned it the hard way.*

She could still smell the fuel from the wrecked plane and
hear the cries of injured passengers calling for help. She remembered screaming for Dee, the other flight attendant.
But Andrea's dearest friend couldn't help evacuate those
injured people, because Dee was a "fatality"—ironically,
the crash's only death. And the cockpit with the flight crew
lay on the other side of the runway. Andrea was on her own.

She'd evacuated all her passengers, survived the fire, and
then taken care of her personal life. Andrea had turned in
her resignation, put the house she'd inherited from an aunt
on the market and updated her résumé. Her parents had
been alarmed by her actions.

"Andrea, are you sure you should quit your job?" they'd
repeatedly asked. "After all, you've been there for five
years.''

"And I've been looking for a change for the last two.
That's why I went back to school.''

"But I thought you wanted to work in a local hospital," her mother had fretted. "Arizona is so far away! You never said anything about a job as a park ranger."

That was true; she hadn't. Strange how she'd ended up outside the Grand Canyon Personnel Office... You could almost call it fate.

The last passenger she'd rescued had been a nine-year-old by the name of Emily. The girl had been flying alone from Denver to the Grand Canyon to vacation with her grandparents. Emily was a lovely child who made Andrea's babysitting task a delight. That delight had ended when an injured Emily was taken from Andrea's arms and placed on a stretcher.

Andrea had stayed close to Emily, first by riding with her to the emergency room in the ambulance, and later with visits to the pediatric ward at Denver Children's Hospital. With a child's typical resilience, Emily had soon bounced back from her frightful ordeal. She'd even regretted the cancellation of her long-awaited trip to the Grand Canyon. Emily had solemnly told Andrea that she'd get on a plane again in a minute if it meant she could go see her beloved grandparents.

Andrea admired the child's courage and devotion to her family. In an effort to help ease Emily's disappointment, she'd made a special effort to buy her a book on the Grand Canyon. So it wasn't surprising that a newspaper ad for Grand Canyon park rangers with E.M.T. certificates had caught Andrea's eye.

On a sudden, inexplicable whim, she'd submitted an application for one of the ten posts offered.

The more Andrea thought about it, the more she coveted the job. She wanted a change of scene; a change from the dull routine of her hometown. She was willing to work anywhere—as long as it was outside. The last thing Andrea wanted was a job indoors. She'd had enough of cramped plane cabins to last a lifetime. Still, she'd never thought anything would come of her application.

To Andrea's amazement, Jim Stevens had called her shortly after for an impromptu phone interview.

His first question was right to the point. "Are you the same Andrea Claybourne who rescued those passengers at Stapleton Airport a few months ago?"

"Yes, I am," Andrea admitted. "How did you hear of that?"

"It made national headlines, Ms. Claybourne."

"Oh. I...I didn't keep up with the news after the crash."

She'd been in too much turmoil, and too much pain at Dee's death. She and Dee had grown up together, they'd attended school together and then they'd joined the same airline. They were inseparable, especially since Andrea was an only child and Dee had no sisters. Dee's death had hit Andrea hard.

"That's understandable," Jim said with sympathy. "Nonetheless, I did read about you. I'd like to know if you're serious about a job as a park ranger."

"I certainly am." Andrea sensed Jim's interest. "I was planning to leave the airline anyway. That's why I went back to school. I'm single, and other than my parents, I have no permanent ties to Denver."

"So your career change isn't a reaction to the crash?"

"Oh, no. Working as an emergency medical technician is a carefully thought-out decision."

"You don't have any problems with flying?" Jim asked. "If we hire you, we'd eventually want to groom you as an E.M.T. for our medivac helicopters."

Andrea paused. "I wouldn't be telling the truth if I didn't admit to having some bad memories associated with flying. But the airline sent me for professional counseling before they'd accept my resignation, and that included getting back on a plane for a short flight. I received a clean bill of health from the counselor. I'm perfectly willing to provide you with his report."

"I'd like that, and I appreciate your candor." Jim sounded pleased. "As a ranger, you'd have to learn the foot patrols, the river patrols and the road patrols before we put you up in the air. You'll also have to get an Arizona driver's license. Does all that sound like something you can handle?"

Andrea felt a growing sense of excitement. "Oh, yes. I'm a good driver and a good swimmer. In fact, my parents own a boat. We spend our summers water-skiing at Sloans Lake."

"I'm glad to hear it. Boating skills are something you'll definitely need. Do you ride? We also have the mule trips down into the Canyon."

"I had equestrian lessons when I was young." Andrea paused. "I've never ridden a mule. It's just the same, isn't it?"

Jim chuckled. "Not exactly, Ms. Claybourne, but it's close enough. Would you like the job?"

"I'd love it! But—" Andrea restrained her enthusiasm. "Mr. Stevens, why me? I'm twenty-six years old with no ranger's experience and only a two-year college degree. I really want this job, but surely there must have been others more qualified?"

Jim Stevens remained silent for a long moment. Then, "You've been honest with me, Ms. Claybourne. I'll be honest with you. A few years ago one of our female rangers died during a river rescue."

"How awful!"

"Yes, it was . . . quite a shock. This particular ranger had the most impressive credentials. She'd been in search and rescue in the military for a while, then worked as a paramedic for the fire department in her hometown. Sarah Wolf's track record was impeccable. But when it came to that river rescue—'' Jim sighed ''—Sarah didn't make it. Neither did the three tourists she was trying to save.''

"That poor woman," Andrea whispered. Life could be cruel. Sarah had drowned, and Dee had died in that crash. Even though she'd been sitting only one seat over, Andrea had never had a chance to help her friend. It seemed no one could help Sarah, either.

"I blame myself for hiring her," Jim went on, his voice harsh. "But how was I to know? She looked great on paper. You may not have much medical or search experience, but thanks to the newspapers, I know you can handle yourself during emergencies. The Grand Canyon Park Service needs people like you—people who don't fold under pressure. We can teach you everything else you need to know, but we can't teach you courage."

At first Andrea didn't know what to say. Finally she spoke in a quiet, measured voice. "I never considered myself particularly brave, Mr. Stevens. I just did my job, the best I could."

"I know that, Ms. Claybourne. And that's why I'm offering you the position. How soon can you start?"

That was two weeks ago. Andrea had packed her bags, given family, friends and little Emily a forwarding address, and loaded her car for the one-way drive to Arizona. It felt strange to be leaving the familiar sights of home, but Andrea welcomed the start of a new chapter in her life.

And now here she was at the Grand Canyon, listening to the shouting inside Jim's office. Well, at least Jim wasn't shouting. Only Kurt was, and his present comments weren't any more flattering than his earlier ones.

"You asked me for my opinion on this batch of trainees, and I'm giving it. They're all acceptable, except for the stewardess."

"That's flight attendant," Andrea corrected loudly, but of course Kurt didn't hear her. He was too busy yelling.

"Jim, I'd never hire a Barbie doll as a ranger!"

Andrea's eyes sparked at the latest insult. The Claybourne women were blessed with a classic beauty. With their Viking heritage they were a striking family, as attested by the fact that two of Andrea's cousins were professional models. Andrea's mother had won a beauty pageant in her own youth, and Andrea herself had been approached by her cousins' employer.

With her tall, willowy figure, blond hair and blue eyes, she was used to men misjudging her because of her looks. But the Claybourne women could also outthink or outfight any man who dared judge them only on appearance. Andrea was no different.

This job was hers. No one was going to take it away from her, especially not a man who was condemning her without a trial, without a chance.

"Come on, Jim, level with me," Kurt insisted. "Is she a relative of the governor or something? Just give me a reason—one good reason—why you hired her, and I'll shut up."

Andrea froze in her seat. She'd asked Jim to keep private the knowledge of her "heroics," as the newspaper labeled them. Her coworkers had saved the clippings for her. Andrea finally looked at them during her required sessions with the airline counselor.

One of the newspaper pictures showed her barefoot in the runway's snow, with Emily bleeding in her arms. The other showed Dee's motionless, white-sheeted form being removed from the burned airplane.

Andrea was embarrassed by the heavy-handed praise accompanying the first photo. As for the latter, it provoked gruesome questions from the morbidly curious. Andrea was deeply disturbed by the sensationalist portrayal of Dee's last minutes by the media, and she'd made a point of telling Jim so.

"Dee and I grew up together, Mr. Stevens. We were like sisters." A fact the media capitalized on, she painfully remembered. For weeks they'd hounded Andrea unmercifully—and unsuccessfully—for details. "I don't want to talk about Dee to strangers. It's been two months now, and I doubt anyone remembers my name from the crash. I'd like to keep it that way, if you don't mind."

To Andrea's relief, Jim had agreed.

Would he break that promise now?

"I'm waiting for an answer, Jim," Kurt demanded. Andrea could hear the impatience in his voice all the way out in the waiting area.

"I'm sorry, Kurt, but you'll just have to trust my judgment as personnel director here for the last twenty years."

Andrea breathed a sigh of relief. It was quickly cut short as the two came into the lobby. Her attention wasn't on the older man, but on the younger. He approached her chair, his brown eyes full of disdain.

"Jim, I trust you, but I don't know about *her*."

Andrea rose to her feet. She met his gaze head-on as he said, "Let's pray she doesn't end up another Sarah Wolf."

CHAPTER TWO

THAT REMARK HAD BEEN made a week ago. Kurt Marlowe, as Andrea discovered was his full name, had stormed away without another word.

Jim was quite reserved. He quickly sent her to the secretary to start the paperwork required by any new job. Andrea suspected that an embarrassed Jim was eager to avoid any questions.

She kept her eyes open, intent on meeting Mr. Marlowe again and giving him a piece of her mind. But not once did she come across the deeply tanned man with the disdainful eyes and mahogany-brown hair. Perhaps it was just as well. She had her hands full learning a new job and settling into her assigned on-site quarters. The last thing she needed as a new employee was to start fighting with her coworkers, no matter how great the provocation. And from the look of the man's strong chin and broad shoulders, he'd probably fight right back.

A few days later, Jim apologized for Kurt's behavior. "You'll have to forgive him, Andrea. Kurt speaks his mind, but we overlook his outbursts for two reasons. One, he's our best floater."

"Floater?"

"Yes. Most rangers are assigned permanent driving, hiking and river patrols. We also have rangers who fly the helicopters and those who train new rangers. Kurt's an expert at all of the above, which is why he has no permanent as-

signment...or permanent partner. We use him wherever we
need him the most.''

"And the second reason?" Andrea asked curiously.

Jim's face grew serious. "Kurt has a very senior position
here at the park. Because of his experience and knowledge,
his opinion carries a lot of weight, particularly when it
comes to training recruits. He can be brusque, even rude,
but don't jump to conclusions. He's paid his dues and then
some. Kurt Marlowe's a damn fine instructor and a valuable man to have around. Just put his comments out of your
mind."

Andrea had tried, but somehow Mr. Marlowe's haughty
face kept intruding into her thoughts. It was a real effort to
buckle down and study the material given to her in class.
Today was proving no exception.

She restlessly crossed her legs, not noticing the appreciative glances from the male recruits. Andrea wasn't used to
sitting for long periods of time. The classroom's hard
wooden desk didn't offer much in the way of comfort, while
the beige summer shorts they were required to wear, starting in May, caused her legs to stick to the seat.

This was just as bad as being in an airplane cabin, she
thought irritably. The Grand Canyon, the most spectacular
riot of color in the nation, was just outside. Thanks to all
her classes, she hadn't even had a good look at it. She'd expected more from her first week of the required sixty-day
probation period.

But that was about to change.

The instructor walked into the room, and the recruits sat
up expectantly in their chairs.

"Trainees, I'm pleased to announce that all of you have
successfully completed the classroom course. Today you'll
be paired up with a seasoned veteran for your outdoor
training. He will remain your partner for the rest of your
probation."

The instructor motioned toward the door. In filed a line of ten rangers, all of them men, and all clad in the same beige shirts, shorts, knee socks and boots that Andrea wore. Unlike Andrea, they also wore their broad-brimmed "Smokey-the-Bear" hats. Hers rested on her desk.

"I'll read the recruit's name first, and then the name of the veteran. You'll pair up outside and stay together for the remainder of your probation. All your assignments will come from your partner. He's your superior, and will have the final say on your evaluation, so treat him accordingly."

Andrea frowned as she saw Kurt Marlowe stride in. He stood apart from the other rangers, his arms folded across his chest. She watched him glance around at the other recruits, then openly stare at her—far longer than good manners permitted. Andrea refused to be intimidated and stared back, lifting her chin with indignation. His eyes narrowed in disapproval, and he turned away, leaving Andrea fuming.

She knew there was nothing wrong with her credentials *or* her appearance. She'd ironed her uniform with meticulous care, making sure the creases were as sharp as those of her flight attendant's uniforms. Her makeup and nail polish were light, and she'd confined her mane of blond hair in a perfectly coiffured French braid.

She noticed with grudging admiration that Kurt Marlowe's uniform was as neatly pressed as hers. He had a clean-shaven face, a military precision haircut, and boots that were polished to perfection. But there was none of the dandy about Kurt Marlowe, Andrea decided. That jawline was too strong, those eyes too calculating. She doubted she'd like him, but she wouldn't underestimate him.

"Randy Wong, your partner is Frank Williams," the instructor continued. "Ted Webster, you'll be working with Felipe Mendez."

Andrea concentrated on listening for her own name—and for Kurt Marlowe's. Under no circumstances did she want him as a partner. She had no objection to working with a man, not that she had any choice in the matter, since all the veterans were men, as were eight of the ten trainees. According to Jim, most of the regular rangers at the Grand Canyon were men. The women tended to fill the helicopter medical attendant positions, like the one she would ultimately have on a permanent basis. However, Jim assured her there were some regular rangers who were women, and Andrea already had a friendly acquaintance with Judy, the only other female trainee in her group.

"Judy Teufel, you'll be working with Dan Prior. Andrea Claybourne..."

Andrea's head immediately turned away from the line of rangers and back to the instructor.

"Your veteran will be Kurt Marlowe."

Not him! Anyone but him! Andrea inwardly cried.

Outwardly, though, she concealed her distress, nodding coolly to her new superior. She hadn't spent the past five years dealing with travel-weary, cranky passengers for nothing. Not for the world would she show any reaction to such a cruel coincidence. Or *was* it a coincidence?

Andrea remembered Kurt Marlowe's disparaging remarks to Jim Stevens, and did a slow burn. If Kurt thought her such a poor specimen and wanted nothing to do with her, why had she been assigned to him? Jim had said Kurt held a senior position. Surely that meant he could make his own choice? Andrea was determined to find out. The last thing she needed was a hostile, rank-heavy ranger as her supervisor.

"Everyone pair up now," the instructor ordered. "And good luck on your first day in the Grand Canyon."

Some of the class clapped and cheered. Andrea contented herself with a smile, then stepped outside into the fresh Arizona air. She wasn't going to hang around like a shy schoolgirl for Kurt to find her; best to get the introductions over with. She easily spotted him in the crowd.

"Mr. Marlowe? I'm Andrea Claybourne. Pleased to meet you." She held out her hand.

"An obvious lie, since you know I don't approve of Jim's hiring you." He took her hand for the briefest of shakes.

"I prefer to be polite instead of brutally truthful," Andrea replied in the controlled voice she'd always used with difficult airline passengers.

"Too bad, because I don't. Mincing words is fine for stewardesses, but it's out of place here."

"Your vocabulary needs some updating. The correct term is flight attendant, not stewardess. However, I wasn't referring to mincing words, Mr. Marlowe. I was referring to good manners. Personally I don't believe they're out of place *anywhere*."

To her satisfaction, Kurt was momentarily ruffled.

"So please, Mr. Marlowe, have your say. Perhaps when you're done we can get down to work."

The barest hint of admiration showed in his face, then was gone. "I don't think you have what it takes to succeed here, Ms. Claybourne. Look at you!"

"You find something wrong with my appearance?"

"No—yes."

Andrea lifted a blond eyebrow. "Which is it?" she asked calmly. "Yes or no?"

Kurt scowled. "You have the height, but there's absolutely no bulk to you."

"Bulk? I don't remember that being a job requirement."

Kurt shrugged, the scowl still darkening his face. "You'll blow away in the slightest breeze. I can't see you carrying a backpack down the Canyon, let alone one end of a loaded stretcher."

Andrea thought of the injured people she'd hauled to their feet on the crashed flight, and the heavy emergency doors she had opened. "Appearances can be deceiving, Mr. Marlowe."

Kurt's eyes narrowed. "It's going to take more than your assurances to convince me."

"I imagine that's what the probationary period is for," Andrea said dryly. "And since you're so dead set against me, why are we working as a team? I find it hard to believe the luck of the draw threw us together."

"You're right, it didn't. I deliberately asked for you, sweetheart, because I intend to put you on the first plane out of here."

Andrea gave him a cold stare. "Please call me Ms. Claybourne, not 'sweetheart.' If I had a dollar for every passenger who called me that, I could have retired to the Riviera."

"Fine. I'll call you whatever you wish." He hooked his thumbs through his belt loops. "Except I won't call you *Ranger* Claybourne, because I doubt you'll last the remaining fifty-three probationary days."

"You're wrong, Mr. Marlowe," she said angrily. "I've burned my bridges to get here. I quit my job, sold my house and left my friends and relatives behind for this position. I'm not going anywhere."

"I think you will," he flung back. "So I suggest you find yourself a new house and go back to your family and stewardess job."

"That's flight attendant. And I'm warning you—" Andrea's voice was diamond-hard with determination "—if you try to sabotage my probation, I'll hire the best sex discrimination lawyer I can afford and haul your *stewardess*-hating behind into the nearest court."

There was a moment of silence.

Then, "I do believe you're serious."

"Try me."

"That won't be necessary. I've never sabotaged anyone's probation yet, Ms. Claybourne. I'm not about to start now."

"How very commendable," Andrea said in clipped tones.

"You'll get the same chance at a ranger's position as everyone else I've ever supervised. You have my word on it."

Andrea looked into his face. There was no mistaking his sincerity; Kurt Marlowe was telling the truth.

"That's all I ask," she said.

"But—"

Andrea knew there had to be a catch. "But?"

"Don't expect me to give you the benefit of the doubt."

She defiantly lifted her chin and gave him a chilly smile. "Don't expect me to want it. Now shall we get started?"

Fifteen minutes later Andrea left her cabin toting a backpack filled with water, food, a first-aid kit and a change of clothes. She didn't know what was in store for her, but she felt a shiver of excitement. This was her first chance to see the Canyon up close. She met Kurt near the South Rim's main trailhead, as instructed.

Andrea paused at the edge of the rim, reveling in the colors of the towering buttes, mesas, plateaus and valleys. A mile below, the snaking Colorado River glinted silver in the sun. A few vacationing tourists and serious hikers passed her, all beginning their journey down to the Canyon floor. Andrea was so engrossed by the view that Kurt had to call her twice before she heard him.

"Do you have everything stowed away inside your backpack? Is your canteen filled?"

Andrea nodded. "I packed exactly what you said. I'm ready when you are."

"Then let's go." They stepped off the paved trailhead and onto the rocky dirt.

"What a gorgeous day!" Andrea couldn't help exclaiming. The sky was a brilliant turquoise, and the temperature in the comfortable seventies.

"You're not here to discuss the weather. You're here to learn."

Andrea bristled at the rebuke, but refused to let him spoil her good mood. "Can't I do both?" she asked.

"I'd rather you paid attention. All new rangers need to become familiar with our trails. The only way to do that is to hike them. Today we'll be hiking the Bright Angel Trail."

"Bright Angel? What a lovely name."

Kurt ignored that. "It's one of only two trails between the South Rim and the river. The Kaibab is the other. These trails are the most heavily used in the park. They're also where most of our medical emergencies occur."

"Don't the mules take these trails?" Andrea asked curiously.

"Yes, and it's a good thing. Sometimes we have to use mules during rescues. They help us evacuate the injured. There's a corral for them on the Rim, another one halfway down and one on the Canyon floor. You'll see the mule caravan later. We'll be hiking down to the bottom today, and back up the canyon tomorrow. We'll pass them en route."

"We're staying overnight at the Canyon's base? You didn't tell me that!"

"What did you expect when I asked you to pack a spare set of clothes?"

"Nothing as good as this." Andrea could barely contain her excitement. She slipped a little on the path, and Kurt grabbed her arm.

Andrea was surprised by his touch. She had an immediate impression of warmth, gentleness and controlled strength. The sensation puzzled her; she'd never experienced such physical awareness of a man before.

"Pay attention to your footing!" he warned her.

Kurt waited until she'd regained her balance, then let her go. Andrea tried to regain her emotional balance as well. It wasn't like her to feel such immediate attraction to a man, let alone one who considered her worthless. It didn't make sense. In fact, it was so confusing that she had to force herself to listen to Kurt's words.

"Bright Angel is the easiest hiking trail we have! It isn't airy at all. If you can't handle this, you might as well pack your bags and go home now."

"Airy? What's that?"

Kurt sighed with exasperation. "Airy means you aren't exposed to the edge. Bright Angel isn't a ridge trail. You won't get as many spectacular, open views, but I won't have to worry about you falling a mile to the bottom, either."

"Don't worry about me." Andrea squared her shoulders. "I intend to reach the bottom just fine."

"You wouldn't be the first rookie to fall," Kurt replied. "At least here on Bright Angel we have two rest houses, plus a halfway ranger station with full facilities. The other trails are much more primitive."

"I can handle it," Andrea insisted.

"The trail's nine and a half miles long," Kurt warned her. "And you're slipping already. Let me know if you get any blisters. Rookies and new boots can be a painful combination. We'll stop at the first rest house and give your feet a break."

"I won't need one," Andrea said as they started down again. "I'm a marathon walker. The New York-London flight used to keep me on my feet for hours." Andrea checked the park signs. The first rest area was a mere mile and a half away, while the second was three miles down the trail. "Why don't we try for the second rest house?"

Kurt didn't look convinced. "We'll see how you do."

She merely nodded, as they headed down the trail. Kurt kept up a brisk pace, and it wasn't long before they'd passed the first rest house. Andrea was aware of his frequent glances; she found herself wondering what kind of man he was. If he wasn't so... so disapproving, he might actually be good company. She'd hate to spend the next two months with someone who found her a burden. Or worse.

It was tough being the new kid on the block. Andrea thought of all the good friends she'd left behind at her old job, and sighed.

Kurt immediately turned around. "Are you all right? I knew we should have stopped back at the first rest area."

Andrea blinked at the concern in his voice. "I'm fine. Why?"

"You sounded tired. Steep descents like this tire out the legs, especially the knees. The next rest area is only about five minutes away. Think you can make it?"

"No problem," she said firmly. "Thanks for asking, though."

But when Kurt turned back to the trail, Andrea saw that he slowed down noticeably. They took the next set of descending loops at a leisurely pace before arriving at the rest area, which had no water or facilities; it did, at least, have a clearing. Kurt found a spot in the shade and motioned for Andrea to join him.

"I thought there'd be more people here," she remarked, glancing around at the handful of other hikers enjoying cold drinks or sprawled in the shade.

"There will be. We don't start to get our big crowds for another month—in early June," Kurt said. "Have a seat, but don't forget to check for snakes. We have rattlers."

"They told us in class," Andrea said, examining the rocks. "It's not something I'd forget." She shrugged out of her backpack, surprised when Kurt took it from her shoulders. "I don't need any preferential treatment."

"I make exceptions on the first day for everyone." He set hers down, then slipped out of his own. "Even stewar—even flight attendants."

She was pleased that he'd corrected himself. It was a tiny victory, but a victory nonetheless.

"Make sure you drink and eat something. Most of our victims suffer from dehydration, so remember to drink as much as you can, whenever you can."

"I will." Andrea sat down on the ground, Kurt taking his own seat a few paces away. She watched as he drank from his canteen. But before she had her own drink, she pulled out a compact and inspected her face.

The canteen stopped abruptly on its way to Kurt's mouth. "What are you doing?"

Andrea's eyes flicked from the mirror to his face, and then back again. "Checking my makeup, of course."

"Unless you're hoping to meet a prospective husband, I hardly think you need it here." Kurt took a swig of water, then continued to watch her.

"And if I think I *do* need it?" Andrea asked in a voice that would have given even the most belligerent passenger pause.

Kurt shrugged. "Seems like a waste of time to me."

"For your information, I'm fair-skinned, so I burn easily. This makeup has sunscreen in it." Andrea touched up her nose and her cheeks. "So does my lip gloss. I have no intention of suffering from sunburn simply because my primping offends you."

Kurt cracked the barest of smiles at her tart response.

"I don't think a complexion that resembles old shoe leather would suit me," she said, glancing pointedly at the weather-roughened skin over his angular cheekbones. Still, on him it looked right, she decided, then felt annoyed with herself. She shouldn't let his appeal—simple chemistry, really—get the best of her. She closed the compact with a loud snap and replaced it in her backpack. She then withdrew a collapsible aluminum cup and unstacked it.

Kurt watched her closely as she poured water into the cup. "You *can* drink straight from the canteen, you know."

"I can drink out of a cup, too." Andrea took a sip, and then another. She pulled a linen napkin out of her backpack, unfolded it and carefully placed it on her lap.

Kurt blinked in disbelief. "A napkin?"

"It's not paper," Andrea defended herself. "It's reusable cloth, so it won't hurt the environment."

"Using *no* napkin would lighten your backpack. Just wipe your mouth on your hand."

"No, thank you," Andrea said primly. "I don't mind carrying an extra ounce or two."

Kurt made a disapproving noise that Andrea simply ignored. He reached into his own backpack. "Would you like some beef jerky?"

"Thanks, but I've brought my own snack."

"This I've got to see," Kurt said dryly. "What is it? Paté? Caviar?"

"Are you making fun of me, Mr. Marlowe?" Andrea removed a plastic container from her pack, and opened the lid. "Because if you are, I want you to know that I won't be baited." She told herself she had fifty-three more days to go, fifty-three more days to keep her cool. And she'd thought the week confined to a classroom had been frustrating!

"Not at all, I only— Is that a croissant?"

Andrea noticed the sudden interest in his eyes, interest that turned to sheer longing when she withdrew a tiny jar of blueberry preserves.

"Yes. I'm sure it's not as filling as your dried cow, but it'll do."

"What kind of woman brings a *croissant* on a hiking trip?"

"You're looking at her," Andrea replied. "I like to pamper myself. After all the airline food I've been forced to eat, I deserve it." She spread the preserves on nice and thick, then took a dainty bite.

"I suppose." Kurt suddenly put away his beef jerky, while Andrea hid a smile.

"Not hungry anymore?" she asked innocently.

"No. I had a big breakfast."

"That's too bad. I have more croissants in my pack. I'm willing to share."

Kurt glared at her. "No, thanks. We have to get going if we want to reach the bottom before the sun sets. Hurry and finish."

Andrea did as he requested, and soon they were back on the trail. Kurt continued his instruction as they descended.

The trail, though narrow, was relatively easy. Andrea followed Kurt, and tried to identify as much of the vegetation as possible. She recognized many of the deciduous and evergreen shrubs, along with the larger Douglas firs. The smaller wildlife, such as squirrels, chipmunks and birds, wasn't difficult to spot.

In her classes she'd been told that the larger animals weren't as readily visible. Deer, coyote, black bear, bobcat, mountain lions and bighorn sheep shied away from humans. The volume of park visitors interfered with the habits of native wildlife; because of this, visitors were required to report rare-animal sightings to the nearest ranger station. Environmental staff kept careful track, particularly of mountain lions, desert bighorn and feral burros to compare with visitor traffic, in an effort to promote the best interests of both animals and humans.

Andrea had never seen any wild animals in their natural habitats. While she wasn't naive enough to think she'd see one on her first day, especially near the more populated rest areas, she was enthusiastic enough to keep looking. Her enthusiasm paid off. About an hour after their break, she noticed movement not far from the trail.

She immediately reached for Kurt's shoulder, stopping him.

"What? Is something wrong?"

Andrea laid a finger to her lips, then pointed toward one of the rare shaded areas off the trail. "Is that a burro?" she whispered.

Kurt peered in the direction she was pointing. "It is at that. You've got good eyes, Ms. Claybourne," he whispered back with grudging approval.

"I was hoping to spot some animals," Andrea said excitedly. "Now what?"

"We see if we can catch it."

"Catch it?" Andrea echoed.

Kurt clapped a hand over her mouth, his fingers warm against her lips. "Not so loud!"

Andrea nodded, and his hand slipped away. "I thought park rules said we only had to *report* feral burros," she said in a quieter voice.

"The *visitors* report the burros. The *rangers* catch them." Kurt removed his backpack and reached into it for a coil of rope, grinning wickedly at Andrea's obvious trepidation. "Trust me, it'll be fun."

"I don't know about this," she murmured, all the while keeping her eye on the patch of color that was the burro. "They never said anything about catching burros in class."

"Are you nervous?"

Andrea lifted her chin to the challenge, but kept her voice low. "Hardly. But Dale Evans I'm not."

"You'll have to learn, Ms. Claybourne. These burros aren't native. They're left over from the Canyon's early prospecting days. They're tough, hardy, and they breed like rabbits. Furthermore, they destroy the vegetation and upset the ecology. Even the cougars can't keep the population in check." Kurt tied a loop in the end of his rope.

"So we have to catch them?"

"Yep."

"Then what?"

"Then we tranquilize them and lift them out by helicopter to a holding area on the rim. The state adopts out the healthy animals to good homes."

"And the . . . unhealthy ones?"

Kurt gave her a telling look.

"Oh, *no!*"

"Our vet is very humane," Kurt assured her. "Now follow me. We're going to get off the trail, so be careful."

"What am I supposed to do?" Andrea asked as she picked her way through the vegetation and around the rocks.

"Just follow my lead. I have a dart gun I'll tranquilize him with. After that, I may need your help with the harness."

"You're going to shoot him?" Andrea frowned. "Can't you just rope him?"

"No. Burros may be small, but they're strong. I don't need this one pulling me over the edge."

Andrea grabbed Kurt's arm, alarmed more for him than for herself. "That hasn't ever happened, has it?"

"No, because we use the dart guns. You'll have to learn to use one, too." Kurt stared down at her fingers.

Embarrassed, Andrea released his arm. "Lead the way."

Kurt continued to advance until they were only yards from the burro. He was close enough to fire, but to their surprise, the burro remained motionless.

"He's only a baby," Andrea whispered. "Oh, look! He's hurt."

"It's a she," Kurt corrected, "but you're right." He studied the burro, gesturing at the bleeding, abraded leg.

"Looks like she took a bad fall. No wonder she didn't run away from us."

"Where's her mother?" Andrea winced as Kurt aimed at the burro's gray-brown rump and fired.

"I hope she's still around. This foal's young enough to be nursing. I'll take a quick look around after the tranquilizer does its work."

Andrea slowly approached as the trembling animal fell to the ground. She ventured a tentative pat on its neck. "She must be thirsty. I wish we could have given her some water."

Kurt shook his head. "It's better to keep her stomach empty. Sometimes the tranquilizers make them sick. You keep an eye on the baby. I'll be right back."

Andrea waited while Kurt did a rapid search of the surrounding area.

"I can't find anything. The mother either abandoned her or..."

Andrea didn't like the sound of that.

"I'd venture to guess this is an orphan," Kurt said. He removed a nylon harness from his pack and fastened it around the burro. "I guess I'd better radio for a copter and evacuate her."

"Wait! Before you call in... They aren't going to—put her down, are they?"

"She's a nursing foal with no mother and an injured leg, Ms. Claybourne. It's the humane thing to do."

"Humane? I think it's a crime! Her leg isn't broken, or she wouldn't be putting weight on it. And I bet she could be weaned to grass and grain in no time."

"Andrea, we're park rangers, not burro-sitters. There isn't enough time or staff to care for all the casualties. I know it sounds cruel, but you'll have to get used to it."

Andrea was too upset to hear the sympathy in Kurt's voice. "I'll never get used to it. I wish I could take her myself."

Kurt opened his mouth, then closed it again. "I've got to radio for that copter," he finally said.

Soon after, the noise of the helicopter blades could be heard. Andrea listened with a heavy heart. She watched as the helicopter dropped a harness and line for the burro. Kurt then fitted the harness around the animal's middle.

Andrea hated seeing the limp, drooping neck as the anesthetized burro was flown away. She watched until it was far in the distance, then lethargically began to coil up Kurt's rope.

"Ready to start back?" Kurt asked.

Andrea swallowed a lump in her throat. "I suppose."

"I'm sorry about the burro," Kurt said. "It's a very unpleasant part of the job. She was a cute one, too. For a burro, that is," he hastily added.

"Yes, she was." It occurred to Andrea that Kurt Marlowe wasn't as tough as he appeared to be.

"I spoke to the pilot and asked him to tell the vet that the baby seemed fairly strong. Once in a while they'll take a chance on a hardy orphan, but usually..." His voice trailed off. "Well, let's get going. There's no sense dwelling on it."

Andrea nodded. She felt tears start in her eyes at the injustice of it all, then forced her thoughts away from the baby burro and blinked hard. She would act as professional as Kurt, at least on the outside. To that end, she concentrated on learning her job as they headed down the trail again.

She wished she hadn't spotted the burro at all.

Kurt was apparently just as determined as she was to avoid the subject. He continued his instruction.

"One of the things you'll need to do when you're hiking is interact with all the people you pass. Smile at them, talk to them, observe them," he said. They were at a wider part of the trail and able walk side by side. "By doing this, we can spot early cases of heatstroke before they become life threatening. Heatstroke is our number one reason for evacuation. Sometimes a rest in the shade and a drink of water can mean the difference between a hiker walking out or being choppered out. And remember, there aren't any phones for hikers to use. They're totally dependent on us to radio for help. So make damn sure the batteries in your radio are always charged."

"They are. They told us that in class." Andrea touched the radio clipped to her belt. "Exactly how hot does it get here?" she asked.

"July's our worst month. Temperatures at the Rim average around eighty degrees, but as you descend, it gets hotter. The Canyon floor can get as high as one hundred six degrees Fahrenheit. When it gets that bad, we start getting victims."

"But I've seen all the park signs warning about the heat! Why won't people listen?" Andrea asked angrily. It was bad enough that burros had to die, but it would be far worse with people.

Kurt shrugged. "Various reasons. Sometimes the victims are foreign tourists who can't read English and don't bother to stop at the main office for foreign-language pamphlets. Sometimes they're just stubborn, or foolish. No matter what the reason, our typical victims don't dress right and don't pack enough water for the higher temperatures."

"I guess I can see how people might not believe the signs," Andrea said. "It's nice and cool now. It can't be more than seventy degrees."

"It is deceiving," Kurt agreed. "But you'll notice the difference as we descend. The heavier vegetation will be replaced by desert species. It'll be in the low nineties when we reach the bottom."

"I didn't realize there was so much desert here. In class the instructor mostly concentrated on search and rescue, and survival techniques."

"That's as it should be, but it doesn't hurt to learn more about the ecosystem. Most people don't know that three of North America's four deserts converge in the Grand Canyon area."

"Three?" Andrea looked up in surprise. "The Canyon is that large?"

"Watch your footing, not me," he rebuked. "And yes, it is. The Grand Canyon is approximately two hundred seventeen miles long, four to eighteen miles wide, and more than a mile deep."

Andrea gave a slow whistle. "No wonder there's room for three deserts."

"It's also why this canyon was named Grand."

"The three deserts?" Andrea prompted.

"The Sonoran Desert runs up through central Arizona. Sonoran plant life, mostly mesquite and acacia, can be found in eastern parts of the Canyon."

"What's the second desert area?"

"The Mohave. It spreads into the western Grand Canyon. You'll get the traditional desert cacti there, such as the chollas and ocotillo. That area's easy to recognize."

Andrea nodded. "And the third?"

"It's along the upper Colorado River. The rim and high elevations of the eastern Grand Canyon are part of the Great Basin Desert."

"If that's the cold-weather tundra desert in Nevada and Utah, there should be sage, pine and juniper," she recited, a bit smugly.

"Yes, and rabbitbrush," Kurt said. Andrea could see he was impressed with her knowledge. "How did you know?"

"I'm from Denver, snow country. I've been to Utah to ski."

Kurt stopped walking, and Andrea did the same. "You won't get much skiing here. Why did a city girl like you ever leave?"

"I was ready for a change." She uncapped her canteen and took a generous swig, not bothering with her aluminum cup. Already the temperature had climbed in the past few miles' descent.

"And that's all there is to it?" Kurt asked curiously.

"Pretty much," she said. The memory of the plane crash and Dee's lifeless face flashed through her mind. Everyone said the tragedy would become easier to deal with as time went on, but Andrea wasn't ready to talk about it yet. "I guess you could say fate had a hand in my decision. Are you from here?" she asked, capping her canteen.

Kurt took a drink himself. When he spoke again, it was obvious he'd accepted her change of subject. "I was born in Phoenix and grew up in Arizona. No brothers or sisters."

"And your parents?"

They started down the trail again.

"They're alive and well."

While he was quite vocal when it came to teaching, Kurt wasn't much for personal conversation. Andrea found it frustrating. She'd heard a little—*very* little—about him through the grapevine. Kurt Marlowe was one of the few people no one seemed to gossip about. Whether it was because of his senior rank or his aloof manner, Andrea didn't know. Either way, she was desperate for conversation to take her mind off the burro, so she pressed on.

"I heard your mother's a botanist who runs her own cactus nursery, and that your father flies helicopters and does traffic reports for a Phoenix news station."

Kurt gave her a sharp look. "Your information is out-of-date. My father recently retired."

"Is that how you learned to fly helicopters for the park?"

"Yes. Dad taught me as a boy."

There was a pause, which Andrea filled by asking, "Did he hope you'd follow in his footsteps?"

"No." Kurt sighed, apparently relenting. "I was more interested in my mother's area of expertise, botany. I decided to major in environmental studies in college. Mother was pleased, but I didn't want to go into the cactus business any more than I wanted to report on rush-hour traffic. So I joined the park service. I wanted a job that would combine flying and the outdoors."

Andrea frowned. "That isn't possible, not really. I flew for five years, and I ought to know. You can't combine flying and the great outdoors. One or the other has to take a back seat."

"I fly quite a bit during the peak summer season. During the rest of the year I'm needed outside. Training is a major part of my duties."

"How long have you been a ranger?" she asked after a moment.

"Ten years. I joined right after I finished college."

That would make him about thirty-two, Andrea calculated.

"Do you think you'll stick with this?"

"You certainly ask a lot of questions. You should focus on your footing instead of my background."

Andrea flushed at the rebuke. She'd been pumping him shamelessly, behavior she usually found offensive in either sex. To make matters worse, she suddenly realized that she couldn't use the burro as her only excuse, either. She wanted to know more about him, plain and simple.

"Concentrate on the Canyon, Ms. Claybourne, and you'll make both our jobs much easier."

Andrea looked away from him, embarrassed. She resolved to limit any further conversation to work-related questions, no matter how appealing she found the subject of Kurt Marlowe.

She gazed out at the gorge below, at the rocky terrain singing with color. Vivid reds, golds, purples... "It's beautiful. I think it's the most beautiful spot in the world."

Kurt stopped his downward progress and turned to face her. "Don't let the Canyon's beauty deceive you. It's also very deadly."

A shiver ran down Andrea's spine, but she refused to allow him to see it. "I know that. I saw what happened to the burro. Its leg—"

"I'm referring to death, Ms. Claybourne. People *die* in this Canyon. Not just animals—*people*."

Andrea was taken aback by the rage in his voice. Yes, the loss of human life was a terrible part of the job, but an experienced ranger like Kurt should know it had to be dealt with. She stared at him openly. His cool exterior gone, his eyes glittering with unreadable emotion, Kurt suddenly seemed a stranger.

"I know better than anyone," he said savagely. "Sarah Wolf was my wife."

CHAPTER THREE

"KURT," ANDREA SAID, using his Christian name for the first time, "I'm sorry. I didn't know."

"I'm surprised. It's common knowledge around here. That, and the fact that I was the one who supervised her training." An awful silence. Kurt's face was filled with such naked pain that Andrea had to look away.

No wonder the grapevine kept so quiet about Kurt, Andrea thought to herself. She'd never heard even a hint of scandal. Even the most voracious gossips would think twice about revealing something so tragic to her, a newcomer.

"Well, don't you want to hear the gory details about Sarah's death? Everyone else did." His voice was harsh, but Andrea could see the anguish in his eyes.

She thought of Dee. She could still remember Dee's smiles and jokes shortly before the crash. She remembered all the others—journalists and coworkers alike—who wanted the "gory details" from her. Their questions had only made a bad situation worse.

"No," she said firmly. "I don't. Reliving all the horror won't bring her back. It's not easy, especially when—" Andrea swallowed hard, an image of Dee's shrouded form in her mind "—when you're unable to change things. My condolences."

Kurt didn't speak, only looked at her with a wondering expression.

"It's almost as if you understand how I feel," he finally said.

Andrea took in a deep, calming breath. "I do—all too well." She saw his sudden curiosity and was aware that he refrained from interrogating her for the same reasons she'd refused to question him. Some things were better left unsaid.

"If you ever need to talk—" Andrea began quietly.

"No," he said in a flat voice. "It's been two years, Ms. Claybourne. There's nothing left to say that hasn't already been said."

Andrea remained tactfully silent. No wonder he'd kept the conversation away from himself earlier.

"Let's go. We have to reach the halfway point by lunchtime."

Andrea nodded, letting Kurt lead the way again. More often than not she found her gaze on his broad back rather than on her footing. So Sarah Wolf and Kurt had been married. That certainly explained some of his overprotective, overcautious attitude. He'd suffered more than just the loss of a coworker. He'd suffered the loss of a wife.

She wondered whether Kurt could have saved Sarah if he'd been present at the rescue site. She wondered whether Kurt blamed himself for not being there. Andrea pitied them both, and in a strange way she envied them. She envied what they'd had, what they shared. She experienced a sudden pang of longing, an awareness of how very alone she was.

None of her relationships ever lasted long. The pilots she occasionally dated carried their authoritative air into their personal lives. Andrea didn't mind taking orders from them on the job, but she drew the line at their high-handed ways off the clock. It was even worse when she dated men outside the airline industry. Once they learned she was a flight attendant, they automatically assumed she was easy sexual prey.

Nothing incensed Andrea more or could be further from the truth. She was tired of men thinking she was a brainless idiot only good for quick physical gratification. Long ago she'd decided she wanted an emotional relationship that came straight from the heart before any man shared her bed. Unfortunately that magic had yet to happen. Until it did, Andrea was content to wait. She spent most of her free time with her friends and family—and slept alone.

But since Dee's death, Andrea had found herself looking at life from a new perspective. She was growing tired of waiting for love to come her way. You couldn't know when your time would run out. So Andrea had decided to live each minute of her life to the fullest. That was why she'd left the airlines for Arizona. And, she now realized, that was why it hurt when Kurt hadn't offered her his friendship.

"How are you doing?"

His sudden question startled Andrea out of her reverie. "I'm . . . fine."

"We're almost at Indian Gardens, the halfway point. If you don't need a rest, we can keep going until we reach it. We should be there in about fifteen minutes."

It didn't take even that long to reach their destination. Andrea craved the shade of the massive cottonwood trees. She took in the Indian Gardens ranger station, campground, and mule corral, but it was the trees that called to her. However, Kurt had other ideas.

"Let's check into the ranger station. There's another couple who started this hike just before us. They should be here by now, especially since we lost an hour or so with that burro. I want to talk to the veteran and see how his rookie's holding up."

With a regretful look at the cottonwoods, Andrea followed Kurt into the small ranger station.

"It's cool inside, too," Kurt said, easily reading her thoughts.

"I know. It's just that I'm so rarely outdoors I hate going in."

"You'll get plenty of outdoor time during the next month, I promise." Kurt smiled at her, the first real smile she'd seen from him.

Andrea was taken aback by the change it made, and again experienced that unwanted tug of attraction. He was a handsome man, but that smile made him positively devastating. He probably hadn't smiled much since Sarah's death, she guessed, even if it *had* been two years.

But Kurt's smile also implied acceptance of Andrea as a coworker, and that was important to her. It meant that for the very first time, she wasn't just Andrea Claybourne, ex-flight attendant, to him; she was Andrea Claybourne, colleague.

That realization created a warm glow inside her. After the experience with the baby burro, and then the shocking news about Kurt's wife, it was a welcome feeling.

Another ranger couple from Andrea's trainee group were waiting inside the station. Kurt made the introductions as the four of them sat down at a lunch table. Andrea had never met the veteran ranger named Dan, but she'd chatted a few times with Judy. In class, Judy's bubbly personality had broken through even Andrea's cautious reserve.

Judy wasn't very bubbly now, Andrea saw with dismay. Her freckled nose was sunburned, her short hair was damp with sweat, and she wasn't saying much. It was Dan who did all the talking as Judy slowly eased into her chair.

"So how's your new partner doing?" Dan asked Kurt, his eyes not on the other man, but on Andrea.

Andrea politely ignored Dan's obvious interest. Even if she wasn't busy trying to learn a new job, Dan's deliberate posturing of his bulky muscles didn't appeal to her. And she didn't care for his outright ogling.

"So far, so good," Kurt said cautiously.

"Andrea looks better than good. She looks fantastic. Judy, you could take a few tips from her. See, not a hair out of place. I approve," Dan said, winking at Andrea.

Judy shrank into her chair, looking even more wilted than before. Andrea felt her own temper rise.

"Judy and I are here to be judged on our performance, not our appearance," she said with a frosty smile.

"You should be used to men admiring your appearance. Weren't you an airline stewardess?"

"The correct term is flight attendant," Kurt interrupted.

Andrea half smiled, delighted with his comment, but when Dan gave her another leering wink, her blood pressure rocketed. Dan couldn't be more blatant if he'd dangled a key to his room! Judy turned away, and Kurt made a sound of distaste. Andrea decided it was time to put a stop to Dan's behavior.

"It's true. I was a flight attendant. The stories I could tell you." She winked back at him, hinting at shared secrets.

Dan eagerly leaned closer. "Please do."

Andrea gave a slow, sultry smile. "I learned the special stewardess walk."

She saw Kurt's eyebrows rise as she used the outdated term.

"I don't think now's the time or place for this, Andrea," he said harshly. "Save it for your time off."

Dan pretended not hear Kurt's order. "Go on, Andrea. Let's hear about the special walk."

Andrea smiled even more. The idiot was walking right into the line of fire. "It's the walk all new stewardesses learn. You see, we have to stand on our feet for hours a day. Have you ever seen regulation airline shoes for women?"

Dan nodded. "Nice, tall high heels, the kind of shoes women ought to wear."

"You're absolutely right. Dan, you are *so* clever."

Dan beamed at the praise, and Andrea continued.

"When trainees work their first twelve-hour flight in those new heels, they end up doing the stewardess walk."

"Tell me about it. Or better yet, show me." Dan was practically drooling.

Andrea dropped her sweet manner. "I'd love to tell you about it. It's when your blisters break and bleed. It's when your nylon stockings rub against the raw sores. It's when you pray you don't cry in front of the passengers before the plane lands. And Dan, if you want a demonstration, why don't you ask your partner for one? That is, if you can get your attention back on her, where it belongs."

There was silence at the table. Judy guiltily ducked her head, and Andrea reached for Judy's hand.

"I know you're hurting, Judy. This isn't an airplane. You can stop anytime you want."

Dan's face turned ugly. "Why didn't you tell me you had blisters?"

Judy flinched, and grasped Andrea's hand even tighter.

Kurt stood up, the chair teetering behind him. "Leave her alone, Dan. You know how much new trainees want to succeed. They always hide problems. You should have noticed!" Then, to Judy, "Come on, let's have a look at those feet. I'll carry you over to an examining table."

"I can walk," Judy bravely insisted.

"For the sake of an ex-flight attendant, let him carry you. It'll do my bunions good." Andrea's teasing tone held just the right note. Judy nodded her agreement, and Kurt threw Andrea a quick look of approval.

He carefully scooped Judy up in his arms and Andrea was struck by his gentleness. She felt a moment of envy.

Andrea and Kurt each removed one of Judy's boots. Andrea cut off both socks, then gasped in dismay at the damage. Kurt's lips drew into a thin line.

"Your feet look pretty bad, Judy," Andrea said, shaking her head.

"Dan, get two mules saddled. You and Judy are going to have to ride back up to the rim. She can't walk."

A chastened Dan nodded and hurried outside to the corral.

"Kurt, why don't you help Dan with the mules? I can take care of Judy."

"I'll do it," Kurt said through clenched teeth, getting out the medical supplies.

Andrea went over to help him, out of Judy's earshot. "Go help Dan! Judy's embarrassed, and she's fighting back tears. She doesn't want to cry in front of you. Please, Kurt, let her have her pride." She impulsively placed her hand on his forearm. The action startled them both.

Kurt suddenly shoved the medical supplies into her arms. "Here. Don't let her walk."

"Shall I leave her boots off?"

"Unfortunately, she'll need them to ride. Put them back on, but lace them loosely."

"All right." Andrea glanced at Judy, who was biting her lip. "Thank you, Kurt."

He gave her a piercing look, then headed for the corral. As the door closed behind him, Judy promptly burst into tears.

"I just know I'm going to get fired," she sobbed. "I really blew it."

"Don't be silly." Andrea unwound some gauze, then cocked an ear toward the door. "If anyone gets fired, it's going to be Dan. Listen."

Kurt's raised voice—and the reprimand Dan was receiving—could be clearly heard.

"His voice sure carries," Judy said, sniffing.

Andrea passed her a tissue. "Kurt does have a temper. You should've heard him tell Jim what a lousy ranger an ex-flight attendant would make. I wasn't even in the same room, but I heard every word."

Judy wiped her eyes. "Well, I'd rather have someone with a loud voice than a big ego. Dan's into bodybuilding. All I heard from him this morning was how much weight he could lift."

Andrea grimaced in sympathy, then started wrapping Judy's feet. "If you're lucky, you'll get a new veteran ranger."

"If I don't lose my job first." Tears threatened again.

"You won't. They'll probably put you on a driving route until your feet heal. Or maybe you'll get to work the front gates and sell admission tickets."

Judy sighed. "Great. I gave up a job as a bank teller to work here."

"Then you'll feel right at home," Andrea said decisively. "Besides, it's better than being in pain. There. All done. I've cleaned, treated, and dressed your feet."

"They feel a little better."

"Do you want to put on some new socks, or have me do it? It might hurt less if you do it yourself."

"I'll do it, Andrea. Thanks."

Andrea got a pair of clean socks from Judy's pack and handed them to her. "Kurt said to loosen the boot laces. But don't make them too loose. You don't want your boots falling off when you ride back up to the rim."

"I've never ridden a mule before," Judy said, wincing as she struggled with the socks.

"Neither have I. But look at it this way. You'll be taking it easy while I've got another five miles of steep trail to hike down today."

"If I had a partner like yours, I don't think I'd mind," Judy said. "You're getting the better deal."

Andrea was silent. If Kurt wasn't so prejudiced against her, she might be tempted to agree.

Kurt and Dan rejoined them a few minutes later to help Judy onto a mule. Dan mounted up, then led Judy's mule from his own. Kurt radioed to the first-aid station on the rim to let them know she was coming.

"I hope she'll be okay," Andrea worried as the mules headed up Bright Angel trail. "She won't get fired, will she?"

"Not over blisters," Kurt replied. "Speaking of which, I want to see *your* feet right now."

"Don't be ridiculous. My feet are just fine. Shouldn't we get going? It's after one already, and we're only halfway down the Canyon."

Kurt pointed at a picnic table behind her. "Sit down and take off your shoes. Or do I have to do it for you?"

Andrea sighed with exasperation. "Oh, all right." She dropped onto the bench, unlaced a boot and yanked off a sock. "Here." She lifted up one bare foot for him to see. "Are you satisfied?"

Kurt grasped her ankle with one hand and lifted her foot up for scrutiny. His eyes met hers in dismay.

"What did you do to these feet?"

"It's not what I did, but what being a flight attendant did," Andrea replied. "Remember the stewardess walk? Airline regulation heels and thin nylons aren't famous for pampering, especially on long flights."

Kurt traced the puckered ridges of a particularly large scar. "It looks like some areas got infected. They must have hurt." He shook his head. "I can't see you doing any stewardess walk with these."

Andrea shrugged. "It was more like the stewardess limp, but I got used to it. We all did." She pulled her foot away from him, embarrassed yet oddly affected by his gentle strokes. "I can assure you, the other foot is just as blister-proof. Compared to my old job, hiking in new boots is a cakewalk."

"Why did you do it?" Kurt asked. "Why didn't you just quit?"

Andrea bent to retrieve her sock and boot. "Because I was young and eager. Because I was tired of school and tired of living at home. I wanted to travel, and make new friends, and meet a prince on a white horse. At the time, sore feet was a price I was willing to pay."

"And now?"

"Except for the sore feet, I still want the same things." Andrea finished laced her boot and stood up.

"Even the prince on the white horse?"

Andrea didn't dare answer that one out loud, especially since her fantasy prince was taking on decidedly familiar features. "I'm ready to go."

Kurt's eyes narrowed. But whatever he might have thought of her deliberate end to the conversation, he didn't press the issue.

The rest of the hike down the trail was without incident. They didn't come across any other injured hikers or rangers, much to Andrea's relief. The burro rescue was more than enough stress for one day. In any event, she was still worried about Judy. Judy had told Andrea in a previous conversation that she was active in outdoor sports as a girl, but was that enough? What kind of skills could an ex-bank teller bring to the Grand Canyon? Judy reminded Andrea of a flight attendant trainee she'd once known—a woman who'd flunked out of flight school. There was a softness about Judy that had nothing to do with sore feet. Andrea felt very uneasy about her prospects.

She wasn't worried about her own performance, however. She was easily keeping up with Kurt, and although he hadn't complimented her, he hadn't criticized, either. On their midafternoon break, he'd refrained from derogatory comments when she'd tidied her hair and snacked on another croissant. She'd been aware of him watching her every move, though. Andrea knew he wasn't about to cut her any slack.

It was late in the afternoon when they reached the Canyon bottom's Pipe Creek rest house near the Colorado River. Andrea picked a shady spot to sit. She closed her eyes and let the water-cooled breeze flow over her face. She knew when Kurt came to sit beside her. In fact, she seemed to be especially alert to his presence.

"How are you?" he inquired.

Andrea opened her eyes and turned toward him. "Good. The air here is so fresh. In the airplane, the cabin was stale, especially with the smokers on those eight-hour overseas flights. I'd get tired just breathing it."

"But you're not fatigued now?"

"Oh, no. Not at all." Andrea took in a contented breath.

"We still have a way to go," Kurt replied. "Bright Angel Campground's on the opposite side of the Colorado. And we still have almost two miles to the suspension bridge to cross the river. Think you can handle it?"

"I'm ready whenever you are."

Kurt nodded. He stood up and held out his hand. Andrea stared at it, then at him.

"Isn't helping me up out of character? I thought you weren't going to give me any breaks."

"Maybe I've reconsidered."

Andrea deliberately crossed her arms and remained sitting on the ground. "Why?"

"Because you spotted a medical problem—a problem I missed—on the first day of the job. Judy could have taken a bad fall with those feet. Dan and I would both be to blame."

"You're admitting you were wrong?" Andrea exclaimed.

"Yes."

"Helping Judy was just doing my job. I don't deserve special treatment for that."

"No, you don't. But for putting Dan in his place, and doing it with style..." Kurt nodded with evident satisfaction, "That scores points in my book. This isn't the first time Dan's tried to play Romeo with a new female recruit. Unfortunately there's far too few women rangers here, and some of the men get distracted. But Dan'll think twice before he ignores Judy again." He continued to hold out his hand.

Andrea took it, and let him help her up. "So you're actually admitting a flight attendant can do something right?"

She had no business indulging in his warm, almost welcoming grasp. He was her instructor. She'd pull her fingers away in a minute, Andrea told herself.

"Ex-flight attendant, you mean. Maybe you'll deserve the title of ranger after all. Judy's lucky you were around."

Andrea again felt that warm glow, the same glow she'd felt when Kurt had first smiled at her. Reluctantly she withdrew her hand, pretending to adjust her backpack.

"I'm glad you aren't the kind of man who judges a woman on looks alone."

"I've always found brains far more attractive than looks, Ms. Claybourne, and you've been blessed with both. If it wasn't for Sarah, I might have given Dan a run for his money."

Andrea took a step back in amazement. "You're joking."

Silence.

Andrea swallowed hard. What had she got herself into?

"Let's go. It's getting late."

Andrea heaved a sigh of relief as Kurt started down the trail. For a minute there, she felt like a rookie flight attendant shaken up by her first pursuing male.

She was used to dismissing shallow men who were all talk and bravado. But she knew with certainty that Kurt Marlowe didn't fit that category. Regrettably, she had no experience with men like him. Men of strong convictions and honor and great personal bravery. He was way out of her league.

And that was what worried her....

CHAPTER FOUR

"I'VE ALWAYS FOUND brains more attractive than looks, and you've been blessed with both. If it wasn't for Sarah..."

Two weeks later, Andrea was still disturbed by Kurt's words. Ever since she'd narrowly escaped death in the crash, she'd thrown herself back into life with a vigor, perhaps too much vigor. Andrea agonized over her attraction to Kurt.

Not knowing if Kurt was attracted to her, too, was very unsettling. Was he warning her off by mentioning his late wife? She was realistic enough to know that might very well be the case, even if he *did* feel something for her.

Andrea decided that the best way to handle the situation was not to say anything. She tried to build a working rapport with him, nothing more, and was pleased to note that she'd made some progress in the past two weeks.

Andrea also spent that time observing Kurt's interaction with others. When he socialized with hikers on the trails, Andrea noticed he wasn't as chatty or as friendly as she was. However, his concern for their safety more than made up for any reserve on his part.

With the other rangers, Kurt was the consummate professional. His expertise was well-known and respected by the staff, and he willingly shared it with others. He might not have had an easy camaraderie with them, but he certainly had their admiration—and Andrea's.

However, Kurt could still be infuriating. They continued to have their disagreements, like the one they were having right now.

"I don't want you near those men," Kurt ordered. "They're drunk, and you could get hurt. I'll take care of this."

"How? By making them mad and getting punched in the nose?" Andrea fired back.

The two of them were responding to a complaint at the Bright Angel campground. What had started as a harmless afternoon barbecue had turned into a rowdy beer blast. The men's loud hoots and hollers heralded more destructive pursuits, and the other campers wanted order restored.

"No one's going to lay a hand on me, not if I can help it," Kurt said. "Now stay here."

"I will not!" Andrea kept pace with him. "As a flight attendant I've had lots of experience with drunks. I'm telling you, if you go in there with an attitude, you're only going to make things worse! They outnumber you, or can't you count?"

Kurt abruptly stopped. "I can count, lady. And, I've done this before."

"I'll bet not as many times as I have, and I'll bet you didn't find it easy."

"Dealing with drunks is never easy." Kurt grimaced in disgust as an empty beer-can fight broke out between two giggling men with very bad aims.

"It is, if you go about it right!" Andrea insisted. "Please, Kurt, let me help!"

Kurt started to fold his arms across his chest, then ducked to avoid a flying beer can. "You want to walk into the middle of that?" he asked incredulously.

Andrea nodded.

Kurt looked from the drinkers to Andrea, and then back again. "Fine. The park service is an equal opportunity employer. Only don't say I didn't warn you."

Andrea let her eyes twinkle. "I won't. Now just follow my lead." She put on her biggest, friendliest smile, and headed over toward the rowdy crew.

"Hiya, sweetheart!" one of the men called out. Whistles and catcalls followed from his friends.

"Hiya, handsome," Andrea replied. "You know, I'm disappointed." There were a few sullen looks and a cry of "Party pooper!" until Andrea added, "You threw a party and didn't invite me. Now, where are your manners?"

There were cheers at this. Andrea stepped over to the picnic table where two backpacks lay. She peered in.

"Just two beers? Is that all? What kind of party is this?"

"It's a summer-break celebration," came one slurred response. "We're tired of college exams and term papers."

Andrea took a seat on top of the picnic table, well aware that Kurt was right behind her. "This is no college party. This is a nursery school party." Her smile took the sting out of the words. "Look, there's no beer, and no girls."

"You're here," one of the men called out. "You can be my girl." He tried to put an arm around Andrea's shoulders, but a hostile look from Kurt quickly changed his mind.

Andrea casually reached for Kurt's hand. Kurt started at her touch, curled his fingers around hers. She scooted closer, boldly leaning against his shoulder. "Sorry, but I already have a date. Where's yours?" she asked conversationally.

One burly student swayed to his feet. "The ladies left. They said they didn't come all this way just to get drunk. But even without them, it's still a great party!" he said belligerently.

The other men grunted their agreement.

"I don't know." Andrea appeared unconvinced. "Really great parties have lots more beer. If I want two beers, my partner here has to go thirsty." She winked at the men. "Now, we wouldn't want that, would we?"

The men looked at one another, their eyes sharing a guilty secret. "We got more," one finally announced.

"Can I see?" Andrea gave them her best "Please, for me," smile.

Within minutes the rest of the beer was out of the tents and piled high on the picnic table. Andrea remained close to Kurt. One of his arms was now resting around her waist, and she felt his hand, strong yet gentle, above her hip.

"Andrea, I'm going to radio for a backup," Kurt whispered in her ear. "This stuff has to be confiscated, and they'll turn ugly when they find out."

Andrea hid her dismay that Kurt was more interested in the scene before them than in her. Her own body had shifted into a higher gear that tracked his every move.

"Let me tell them," she whispered back, forcing her mind back to her work. To the men, she announced loudly, "I take it back. You guys certainly do know how to throw a party."

There were rousing cheers and high-fives among the students. "Have a beer, Ranger!" one of them called out.

Andrea studied the tower of stacked six-packs. "I have a better idea. Why don't we save this for later? We can have another party—a better party—when the girls come back."

This suggestion was met with mixed reactions. Kurt moved protectively closer, but Andrea remained on her perch on the table. "In fact, my partner and I will save it for you at the ranger station."

"You're a party pooper, after all, aren't you?" one of the men whined.

"I'm afraid so, guys." Andrea looked up and saw that four other rangers had arrived at the campground. "But I'm a nice party pooper. If I wasn't, I'd arrest you for being drunk and disorderly." That much was true. Rangers were empowered to do so. They made a few sporadic narcotics and alcohol arrests every summer.

"I could also take your beer and donate it to the nearest trash station."

There was a loud chorus of groans.

"But if you agree to clean up this mess you made, and go back to your tents for the rest of the day, I'll save your drinks for later."

"How much later?" the belligerent man asked.

His buddy said, "Shut up! You wanna go to jail?"

Andrea waited until it was quiet again. "These four other rangers are going to move your beer to a safe spot. In the meantime, I see lots of empty cans on the ground. Let's get started, shall we?"

There was some grumbling and stumbling as the men slowly began to clean up their mess. The other campers broke into applause at the sight. Andrea gave them a slight acknowledging nod and allowed herself to savor the moment.

Then, despite wishing to prolong Kurt's staged embrace, she hopped off the table and turned around to face him. "It was a piece of cake," she couldn't resist saying. "Just like I told you."

Kurt was plainly astonished. "I don't understand. How did you manage?"

Andrea waved her hand in a disparaging gesture. "This was nothing compared to the charter flights I used to do for football fans. Those people were *real* guzzlers. And don't forget the late-afternoon businessman's specials. Two cocktails for the price of one on all commuter shuttles." Andrea shivered. "Those jaunts were a real education. Frankly, I thought I'd left all that behind. I hope we don't get bouncer duty too often."

"If we do, I'll make sure I have you with me. That way, both our noses can remain unbroken." Kurt offered her one of his rare smiles, and suddenly the applause of the other campers seemed meaningless in comparison.

Twenty minutes later order was restored. The beer was gone, the campground spotless, and the revelers were in their tents sleeping it off.

"They aren't getting their beer back," Kurt warned as he and Andrea hiked out toward Phantom Ranch, their original posting for the day. "Not if I have anything to say about it."

"That's fine with me. You're the senior ranger. Those students will just have to understand you pulled rank on me." Andrea grinned. "If they even remember half of what I said."

"Probably not even that much."

"You know, Kurt, I can't believe people would come all the way to the Grand Canyon and hike seven miles to the bottom just to get drunk."

"Usually drinking problems are at the campgrounds above the rim, not on the bottom," Kurt explained. "Alcohol is allowed at all national parks, and there are authorized vendors on both the rim and the Canyon floor. Unfortunately, some people are more interested in the booze than in the scenery."

"They should just stay home," Andrea declared.

"My sentiments exactly. In fact, if it were up to me, I'd ration the number of people allowed into the Canyon."

"You're not serious!"

"Oh, but I am. Of course, that's just my personal opinion. It's not what we're supposed to teach our trainees." Kurt stopped under some shade, and waited for Andrea to join him. They both sat down after checking for crawling pests.

"You'd actually limit incoming people, Kurt?"

"Why not? Some of the other major parks do. We get forty thousand visitors a day during the peak season. We have traffic jams, flight pattern stack-ups, and not enough parking, hotels, and restaurants in the area to accommodate everyone.''

"But that's just during the summer, isn't it?"

"The damage the Canyon suffers during the summer lasts all year, Andrea! Did you know that out of four species of previously endangered plants in this canyon, two are already extinct?"

"No, I didn't," she reluctantly admitted.

"And the other two are on the brink," Kurt said impatiently. "Letting in so many people is harmful to the ecology. You should know that. Didn't your classes teach you to treat any water you drink?"

"Yes."

"Well, it wasn't always that way. The mob of visitors has fouled the Colorado River and its side streams. The water's undrinkable now without purification tablets."

"I agree it's a shame. But you can't close the Canyon! If you did, you'd deny the state needed revenue and you'd deny hardworking people the opportunity to see one of the greatest sights in the world. And you couldn't classify the Canyon as a national park, which means it wouldn't be eligible for federal grants."

"The Canyon existed for years without federal money," Kurt argued.

"Yes, and according to my classes, the Indian ruins were vandalized, feral burros ran wild and destroyed the delicate balance of plant life, and people came to the Canyon anyway. At least the government provides for some sort of regulatory force—us."

"That's such an idealistic view," Kurt said irritably. "In fact, it's the typical party line around here. Well, I personally think the fewer people allowed in here, the better."

"I'm surprised you even continue working here, then."

Kurt's response was surprising. "I've been repeatedly offered a position with a Canyon environmental protection group. Environmental studies is my specialty, and heaven knows the Grand Canyon needs protection. I can't say I haven't been tempted, but—'' He shook his head.

"But?"

"Someone needs to protect the people in the Canyon, too. I admit that, and I know I can do it." He sighed heavily. "Did your classes tell you know how many victims we had last year, Andrea?"

"I—I don't remember. A hundred maybe?" she guessed.

"Wrong. Over a thousand."

"A thousand?" The number was staggering.

"Yes. Roughly speaking, nine hundred victims were dragged out by mules. One hundred were flown out by helicopter. Ten we took out by stretcher. The remaining five— our alcohol-related drownings—made it out in body bags." Kurt glanced at Andrea's shocked face. "What's worse, we get the same statistics every year. You can ask any ranger who works here."

Andrea was silent for a moment. "I believe you. But Kurt, I still can't agree to locking everyone out. That's like taking great works of art out of museums and hiding them in cellars. People have a right to enjoy beauty."

"Do they have a right to endanger themselves, the plant and animal life, and to foul the waters?"

"No, of course not. But why ruin it for everyone because of a few rotten apples?"

Kurt rose to his feet in disgust. "I should have known better than to argue environmental issues with a—" He abruptly broke off.

"With an ex-flight attendant? With someone who catered to tourists?" Andrea finished.

"I didn't say that," Kurt said immediately.

"No, but you thought it!" Andrea stood quickly, hiding her hurt.

"Andrea, you don't understand!"

"You're wrong. I understand perfectly. I'm smart enough to pacify drunks, but not smart enough to have an opinion of my own." She was mortified that her voice nearly broke on the last words. She was such a fool! She should have guessed Kurt hadn't truly accepted her. And she shouldn't let that fact upset her so much.

"Andrea, wait!" Kurt called as she started down the trail without him.

"Why? Are you afraid the dumb stewardess will get lost?" she flung back, refusing to stop. "I've hiked here for two weeks. I think I can find my way back without you."

"Would you slow down? You're going to break a leg," he yelled, running to catch up. He grabbed her arm. "I didn't mean to hurt your feelings."

"Don't flatter yourself. I'm angry, that's all. Now let me go."

Kurt did, and Andrea fought to control her emotions.

"I don't want an unfortunate slip on my part to ruin our working relationship," Kurt told her. "Please accept my apology."

"I'd rather you allowed me to speak my mind about the Canyon."

"You're wrong, Andrea. I know what I'm talking about."

"This Canyon belongs to everyone, not just you."

"I know what's best for it!" he stubbornly insisted.

"In that case, the sooner you take that job with the environmental protection group, the better. It seems to me, *Ranger* Marlowe, that you're on the wrong side of the fence."

"Maybe I am, but I sure as hell don't need some rookie telling me so." Kurt stomped angrily down the trail, leaving her to follow or stay behind, as she pleased.

After a moment, a trembling Andrea followed. She and Kurt were to rendezvous with Judy and Dan at Phantom Ranch.

Phantom Ranch provided the only services below the rim for both hikers and riders. Segregated male and female dorms with showers could be rented for a small fee, while private cabins were available for those who wished more luxury. Food and other supplies could be bought, and there were a number of places for wading and swimming.

Hikers, as well as mules, took one day to make the trip down, and another to make the trip up. Phantom Ranch was a much-needed overnight retreat, and it was here that Andrea and Kurt would spend the night.

They both needed the rest. They'd hiked down Bright Angel Trail earlier that day before being dispatched to the campground, while a recovered Judy and her partner had ridden down the Kaibab on the mules. In the morning, they planned to switch; Andrea and Kurt would ride up with the mule caravan while Dan and Judy would hike.

In the meantime, all four of them would spend the night at the ranch. Fortunately cabins were still available this time of year. The women would have one to themselves, as would the men.

Andrea tramped into Phantom Ranch with a heavy heart. She'd been looking forward to her first mule ride, and now her eager mood had been ruined. Her spirits lifted a little when she saw all the mules in the corral. The caravan hadn't arrived yet when she'd left to handle the complaint about the beer drinkers. Now Judy was here. It would be nice to have someone else to talk to—someone who didn't begrudge her an honest opinion. Andrea hurried to her assigned cabin, coolly nodding to Kurt as he watched her progress from the porch of his own.

"Hi, Judy. It's good to see you again!" she immediately sang out. "I haven't seen you since your last mule ride."

"Don't remind me," Judy groaned, arching her back. She was barefoot and sprawled on her bed. "I had aches in the worst places then, and they're just as bad now." Judy shifted and rubbed her bottom. "Thank goodness it'll be you on those smelly beasts tomorrow, and not me."

Andrea gave her a sympathetic smile and sat down on the room's one chair. "I think they're kind of cute. They have such long eyelashes compared to horses."

Judy rolled her eyes. "You always look on the bright side, Andrea. Just wait until it's your turn. You'll be saddle-sore like me. I wish they had hot baths here instead of showers."

"How about a nice long soak in the water?" Andrea suggested. "If we hurry, we can beat the rest of the crowd. I know a shortcut to a bathing pool."

Judy looked up in surprise. "You do?"

"Oh, yes. It's definitely one of the advantages of being a ranger and learning all the trails. You have a bathing suit, don't you? We're all supposed to pack one."

Judy nodded.

"Then let's change. I feel positively grimy."

"First let me grab some aspirin, then I'm right behind you."

Sure enough, Andrea and Judy had the pool to themselves. A small rocky hollow with gently flowing water provided a shallow place to sit and relax.

"This certainly beats fighting the crowd for the showers," Judy said, cupping water to wet her shoulders. "I'd rather save what energy I have to crawl into bed."

Andrea frowned. "I'm surprised you're still getting so tired. Didn't the driving patrols rest your feet? How are they feeling?"

"My feet are fine. As for the rest of me, I haven't been hiking for two weeks like you. I've been sitting in a Jeep. I'm just not in shape yet."

"I suppose." Andrea undid the French braid she usually wore, and let her hair hang free down her back. "Well, it'll be the weekend soon, and you can relax then."

"I have to work." Judy threw Andrea a curious glance. "Don't you?"

"No. I never have to work weekends."

"Never?" Judy echoed. "But weekends are the park's busiest times. All the rookies have to work them."

"Funny, I never do."

"Lucky you," Judy said enviously. "My days off are during the week, and they're never together."

"I suppose it's because Kurt gets weekends off that I do," Andrea said slowly. "It wouldn't make sense for us to have different days off."

Judy nodded. "That's probably it. Your instructor does have enough seniority. I only wish Dan did. We get stuck with Tuesdays and Thursdays off. That's not enough time for me to go anywhere. I certainly can't go home and back in one day."

Andrea suddenly wondered where Kurt went on *his* days off. Odd how Andrea never saw a trace of him on weekends, although he lived in the same ranger quarters that she did.

"Andrea?" Judy prompted.

Andrea realized she wasn't listening, and reluctantly put away the intriguing subject of Kurt's weekend whereabouts. It really wasn't any of her business, she told herself.

"Sorry, Judy, I was wool-gathering. Speaking of your partner, how's Dan treating you?"

Judy smiled then. "Not too bad, considering. Thanks to Kurt, Dan's bent over backward to help me. I only wish I'd been able to talk him out of today's mule ride."

Andrea saw Judy shiver, even though neither the water nor the evening air was cold. She splashed more water over her arms as Judy said, "Did you know the mules like to walk on the very edge of the trail?"

"The edge? Near the drop-off?"

Judy nodded. "Yes. No matter how many times you rein them over, they just plod right back to the edge. The mule-team driver said you can't make them walk any different."

"How strange. I wonder why."

"Mules have eyes on the sides of their head," Judy said dismally. "The wall looks like an obstacle to one eye, so they shy away from it. I know. I asked."

"Well, I imagine their other eye can see the drop-off. I've never, ever heard of a single mule slipping and falling, not even on an airy trail, so—" Andrea shrugged "—I'm not going to worry."

"I didn't like it. I hate the heights, Andrea."

The admission was so surprising that Andrea froze, the water draining from her cupped fingers. "You're afraid of heights?"

"No, not regular heights. Just…just being on a mule that keeps getting closer to the edge of a long drop." Judy shivered again. "I'll take blisters over mule rides any day."

Andrea dropped her hands into the water again and tapped out tiny ripples. "Aren't you happy in this job, Judy?" she asked softly.

"I—it's so hard, Andrea." Judy managed a wan smile. "Once I get used to it, maybe things will be easier."

"You could always leave," Andrea suggested. "You could go back to the bank. There's plenty of other jobs a smart woman like you could do."

"I know, but I hate to quit. Especially when Dan doesn't think I have what it takes to be a ranger."

Andrea could certainly understand that, but still—

"Judy, why did you ever take this job?"

"Man trouble." Judy hesitated, then blurted out the truth. "My boss fell in love with me, and he was married. He wouldn't leave me alone when I told him I wasn't interested. I guess you could say I ran away from home. Silly, yes?"

It was more than silly, Andrea thought to herself. It was downright frightening. "Judy, why *this* job? Why here?"

"I wanted to be someplace my boss couldn't reach me. I know a friend of a friend who works here, and he said they needed more women to meet their quotas. I told you I was pretty athletic in school, except for riding mules, that is, and I've always loved camping and stuff. Everyone thinks I'll make a good ranger."

"And you, Judy? What do you think?"

"I'll catch on soon. I'm just a slow starter." Judy hugged herself, then stood up. "It's getting close to dinnertime. I'm supposed to meet Dan at the chow hall. Want to join us?"

"I'd rather stay here for a while." Andrea could never get enough of the outdoors. "I'll see you back at the cabin, okay?"

"Okay."

Andrea watched the other woman leave. Poor Judy, she thought as she stretched out her legs and tipped back her head, resting her weight on her arms. The water lapped at the waistline of her one-piece maillot and wet the ends of her hair.

How could anyone consider living in a place like this a chore? Andrea gazed up at the Canyon walls growing purple with the fading light, the towering buttes casting black shadows against the colored rock. A mile up, the last rays of sun filtered through; they bounced off the water, making tiny stars in the ripples.

She'd never leave all this. *Never.*

Her reverie was interrupted by the sound of a voice. Kurt's voice. "Aren't you going to have dinner?"

Andrea looked up and saw that his hair was damp from washing, and he'd changed into fresh clothes.

"Of course," she replied, sitting straight up again.

"When?"

"Maybe later. Judy told me we were invited to eat with them, so feel free to go without me. I'm sure Dan's waiting." After first enjoying Kurt's staged embrace at the campground, then arguing with him, Andrea had resolved to maintain a more even keel. She vowed to act as professionally as possible. As a result, her words came out sounding abrupt.

Kurt wasn't put off. Instead of leaving, he took a seat on one of the larger rocks around the pool. "I've already been told I'm not welcome. It seems *Dan* Juan wants Judy to himself."

Andrea gave him a sideways glance, then turned her attention back to the Canyon walls. "You ought to go eat with them for that reason alone. Judy deserves a break."

"Oh, I don't know. After their rocky start, it seems Judy doesn't think Dan's that bad after all." Kurt shrugged. "With so many men to choose from, sooner or later the women find someone to date. Except for you. You don't seem very interested in a workplace romance."

"How very fortunate for the rest of the staff, considering my past work experience and unfavorable views toward the environment," Andrea replied with uncharacteristic sarcasm.

"I didn't say that."

She looked at him sharply. "Not in so many words, but you managed to get the message across, nonetheless."

"I did apologize," Kurt reminded her.

Andrea remained silent, staring moodily at the water.

"Damn it, Andrea, would you look at me?"

Andrea wouldn't, fervently wishing she'd kept her mouth shut. She closed her eyes, then opened them again at the sound of splashing. Seconds later his hands were on her upper arms, lifting her to her feet.

"Kurt, your boots!" she exclaimed. He was up to his calves in water, and she was dripping all over his fresh clothes. "You're getting soaked! Let go of me!"

Kurt's answer was to pull her even closer. "I never meant to hurt your feelings, Andrea."

Their eyes were only inches apart. Andrea could read the sincere contrition in his. Then that contrition was replaced by something else, a strange, sweet something she couldn't help responding to. His lips met hers. Her arms wound around his neck. Then she was held tight against his chest. She closed her eyes and savored his kiss.

A tiny sound begged for release in Andrea's throat, then was forgotten as she gave herself up completely to Kurt's embrace. One of his hands traced a slow, sensuous path down her wet spine, while another found refuge in her long hair.

Hurt feelings were replaced by wondrous, exciting sensations. Andrea could have stayed in his arms forever....

But it was Kurt who first broke the embrace, Kurt who dropped his arms and backed away. She gasped at the outline of her wet body clearly imprinted on his clothing. The sight was so suggestive, so irresistibly compelling, that she had to turn away to regain control.

Kurt misinterpreted her action. "Andrea, I'm sorry. I didn't mean for that to happen," he said intently. "I've reprimanded enough other male rangers for this. I..." For the first time Andrea saw Kurt at a loss for words. "I mean—I just wanted you to know you're entitled to your own opinion."

Andrea nodded. "I understand," she managed to blurt out, unable to keep her eyes from him for long. "Let's just blame it on the sunset."

But it wasn't the sunset that had made Andrea return his caresses. It wasn't even simple, physical chemistry. It was something else she couldn't quite put a name to yet. An-

drea watched as Kurt backed out of the water, his gaze on
her all the while. He reached the bank, and the two of them
stared awkwardly at each other. Andrea finally decided it
was up to her to rescue them, and desperately racked her
brain for a solution.

"While we're on the subject of opinions, may I voice another?"

"Yes?"

"I'm worried about Judy. I know that Dan and Jim
Stevens are the best judges of her abilities, but she seems
so—so—"

"So what?"

"I don't know—lost is the best description, I suppose. I
know I'm just a rookie myself, and I still have to prove my
own abilities," Andrea said in a sudden rush of words, "but
I'm worried about her."

Kurt seemed unable to concentrate on the subject. "What
do you want me do, Andrea? Talk to Jim?"

"No, not that," Andrea said quickly. "But would you ask
Dan to keep a close eye on Judy until she's more comfortable with her job? I'd ask him myself, but Dan and I aren't
exactly on the best of terms."

"No, you certainly aren't. Unlike—" He broke off.

For a moment Andrea thought he was going to refer to
what had just happened between them. Instead, Kurt said,
"I'll talk to Dan for you after dinner."

Andrea breathed a sigh of relief, glad for once that Kurt
wasn't one to talk about personal matters. "Thanks. I appreciate it."

"Speaking of dinner, are you sure you won't join me?"

Andrea almost wavered, but she didn't trust herself to
remain calm in his presence, especially while he still wore her
body's imprint on his clothes. She sank back down in the
water with shaking legs.

"No, thanks. I'm still cooling off." That was true in more ways than one. "You go ahead."

Kurt bent over and retrieved something from a dry spot of ground. "Here. I brought you a towel and a flashlight." He set them next to her sneakers.

"You didn't have to do that!" Andrea said, surprised at his thoughtfulness.

"I don't need my rookie catching pneumonia or breaking a leg in the dark. I'll see you in the morning. Good night."

Andrea watched his departure with relief and regret—relief that his enticing arms were no longer around her willing body.

And regret—for the same reason.

CHAPTER FIVE

"ALL RIGHT, EVERYONE, mount up! Anyone who needs help, raise your hand!" yelled out the mule-team driver. "Don't be too proud to ask. Not everyone's been raised around these animals, and they can be ornery."

"You wouldn't be ornery for me today, would you, sweetheart?" Long, equine eyelashes blinked as if to say, "Who, me?" and Andrea smiled. She rubbed the nose of her assigned mount, then checked the tightness of the saddle cinch.

It was just after sunrise, yet Phantom Ranch was alive with activity. Last night's riders were scurrying out of their beds and down to the corral for the ride back up the South Kaibab Trail. Andrea had done some scurrying herself. Between reliving Kurt's kiss, worrying about Judy, and the excitement over her first Canyon mule ride, she'd fallen asleep far later than she'd planned. Consequently she'd overslept and had to rush to pack, make chow hall, and get to her mule on time.

She hadn't seen Kurt this morning. Despite her frenzy of activity, she caught herself looking for him. After all, she excused herself, he *was* her partner. She should keep track of him. She didn't find Kurt, but she did spot Judy at the corral.

"Hi, Andrea. I tried to wake you, but you were fast asleep. I'm glad you made it."

"So am I. Kurt would have a fit if I missed my ride." She glanced around. "You haven't seen him, have you?"

Judy shook her head. "No. He didn't eat breakfast with me and Dan."

"Oh. Well, I'm sure he'll show up. Good luck on the hike today. I'm glad I'm riding."

"Not me." Judy wrinkled her nose. "Awful, smelly beasts. See you tonight up on the rim."

Andrea waved goodbye with a thoughtful expression on her face. The mules didn't smell any worse than any other outdoor animal. In fact, they were clean and healthy, their shiny coats indicative of frequent grooming. Again, Judy seemed to see only the negative.

"Don't you listen to her, precious." Andrea scratched behind the long, silky ears of her mule. "She doesn't know what she's talking about. *I* think you're gorgeous."

"Strange words to hear about a mule."

Andrea brightened at the sound of Kurt's voice. "Perhaps." She turned to greet him. "Good morning, boss."

"Sleep well?"

"Like a baby," she fibbed. "I'm packed and ready to go."

"Do you need any help mounting up?"

"Oh, no. I know how to ride." To prove it, she untied the reins from the hitching post, gathered them in her hands, then easily swung herself into the saddle. Her mule stood patiently, long ears flicking backward and forward.

Kurt watched her adjust the stirrups. "I'll be bringing up the end of the mule caravan today. I want you directly in front of me, so let everyone else go by first."

Andrea nodded, gently stroking the mule's neck. "Anything else?"

"A few things. The mules have their own routine. They've made this trip numerous times, so once we're underway don't try to control your mule. Just let him follow the one in front."

"Got it. I put him on automatic pilot."

"Exactly. Many first-time riders are tempted to rein their mules away from the edge of the trial."

"I won't. I know they like being close to the edge."

"I didn't know they taught that in class," Kurt said, raising his eyebrows.

"They don't," Andrea said. "I heard it from Judy."

"Dan told me she was nervous."

"Well, I'm not nervous around heights, and I'm not afraid of mules. I intend to sit back and enjoy the ride. Just out of curiosity, why don't they use horses, or even burros? It would make more sense to use all the feral burros they capture here than adopting them out."

"The burros are too small for most of the male tourists. As for horses, they get too... amorous."

"Amorous?"

"Yes, and these trails are too narrow for an excitable stallion or a skittish mare in heat. Mules result from cross-breeding a male donkey and a female horse. They're always sterile, and such, they make for better, calmer mounts. We've never had a mule-related death at the Canyon."

"That's good to know."

"I'll be right behind you, so if you have any problems, just shout." He frowned. "You should have riding gloves. Wear them."

"My hands are just like my feet—blister-proof. Serving the first one hundred airline dinner-trays took care of that," she said, but she pulled out her gloves anyway and put them on.

Kurt waited until she was finished, then headed briskly toward his own mule. Andrea found her eyes following him. He certainly hadn't bothered with much idle conversation this morning, she thought regretfully. He hadn't even given her a lingering glance.

"Single file, everyone. Let's head out!" the mule-team driver yelled. One by one, the fifteen riders obeyed.

Andrea pulled into the fourteenth slot, with Kurt bringing up the rear. They easily covered the distance out to the Colorado River and crossed the Kaibab Suspension Bridge. Then they were on the steep climb up.

Her mule had a comfortable, rocking gait, and Andrea was able to relax in the saddle. The sign at the bottom of the trail indicated that they would climb 4,780 vertical feet, and the mule-team driver announced they'd arrive at the top of the South Rim between two and four in the afternoon. A brief rest-stop at the Tonto Formation was scheduled; when they arrived there, box lunches would be distributed.

She adjusted her hat against the sun and settled in for the ride. Andrea was acutely aware of Kurt behind her. More than once she could feel his gaze as she observed the scenery. Well, if he was waiting for her to fall off, he was going to be disappointed. She might not have ridden for years, but once you learned, you never forgot.

Not only that, the mules provided an added bonus. As Andrea didn't have to worry about her footing, she was able to pay full attention to her surroundings. The Canyon had a different personality viewed from the bottom up, although the colors were no less breathtaking. Andrea once again found herself wishing that her regulation backpack allowed room for her camera. Perhaps on her next day off, she mused, she could take some photographs.

She was surprised when the mule-team driver signaled for everyone to stop. She turned around to Kurt for confirmation.

He nodded. "I know it's early for lunch, but the Tonto Formation is the only place to rest on the way up. There's no room for the mules to stop anywhere else. Wait for dismounting instructions."

Andrea nodded. Minutes later, she and Kurt were enjoying their lunches.

"This meal should really be called brunch," Andrea observed.

"Better now than never," Kurt returned. "We aren't allowed to eat while riding. There's less chance of dropping litter on the trail that way. Besides, the less experienced riders need to pay attention to their seats."

"I'd rather take pictures than eat. Look at all the different colors of rock—the pinks, greens, and look at that brown.... I wish I had my camera."

"All the new rangers say that," Kurt replied amiably. "After a while you'll be able to match the colors to their specific geological layers."

"The instructor went over them in class, but I'm afraid I can't remember them all," Andrea admitted ruefully as she gathered up her food wrappings.

"It isn't hard to learn. The Grand Canyon has nine basic rock layers. The Tonto Formation is made up of three of those."

"Which one is the pink?"

"It's called Muav limestone. The green is Bright Angel shale, and the brown is Tapeats sandstone. They make up the bottom layers here. Remember them, and you know one third of the Canyon's composition."

Andrea repeated the three layers in her head. "And the others?"

"The top six layers are also made up of shales, sandstone and limestone."

"Those are the main building blocks of the Canyon?"

"Yes."

"And the names of the remaining six? Isn't one of them called Kaibab?"

Kurt nodded, swallowing a bite of apple. "They're easier to remember if you split them in half and take them out of order. Temple Butte, Hermit and Redwall are named after natural formations. The remaining three—Supai, Coconino and Kaibab—have Indian names."

Andrea frowned. "I should write them down for future reference."

"You won't need to. You'll learn them after the first hundred or so park visitors ask you to identify the names, colors and dates of the different layers."

"Dates? I have to know dates?"

"Just rough ones, like which rock is Precambrian or Mississippian, Devonian..." Kurt's eyes twinkled.

Andrea groaned. "I can tell this is going to be like learning the drink menu for the airline. The passengers would ask me to reel off all the items and prices on the liquor list, then they'd settle for a ginger ale." Andrea calculated out loud. "Let's see. That's nine rock layer names, plus dates, colors and specific rock types." She brightened. "Thirty-six. Not too bad. The drink list was longer than that. Run those by me again," she urged Kurt.

"I will when we reach the South Rim. For the rest of the ride, just concentrate on observing the different layers. Many of them are quite distinctive in their appearance. With a little practice, you should be able to pick out where one formation ends and the next starts. You won't need names for that."

"Thanks, Kurt." She gave him her first real smile of the day.

Kurt's eyes were friendly as he rose to his feet and took the remains of both their lunches to the trash bags. "Well, at least you *want* to learn. That's more than I can say for some of my rookies."

"You can never be too prepared," Andrea said. Her face grew pensive as she thought of Dee. Dee had been trained for all emergencies, but it hadn't helped.

"Anything wrong?" Kurt asked.

"No." Andrea shook off the memory. "It looks like everyone else is finished eating," she said quickly. "I'd better get back to my mule."

The sun broke through the morning clouds as the mule caravan got underway again. Andrea basked in its warmth, but it wasn't long before she was reaching for her canteen. The mules slowed to a more plodding pace in the heat. Other riders, especially those without hats and sunglasses, began to look flushed.

Soon Andrea, too, began to wish for some shade. The Kaibab was an airy trail, so they couldn't even pull over to cool off. It was so narrow, in fact, that any hikers also using the trail were required to climb up above the footpath, remaining precariously perched until the mules passed.

Every so often Kurt would call out, "How are you doing?"

At first Andrea would turn around in her seat and answer, but now she was just waving her hand at him. Not enough rest and the oppressive heat were taking their toll. She felt listless and sleepy, and had to force herself to stay alert. To accomplish that, she started concentrating again on the rock layers Kurt had described.

She deliberately focused on the different formations, reviewing their names in her head. She also kept her eyes swiveling at all times. She might not feel wide-awake, but at least she would look it to Kurt's critical gaze. Andrea stifled a yawn. To check the mule's upward progress, she glanced straight down over the edge—and froze.

There was someone down there on a narrow ledge! She could just see the top of his head. Andrea frantically looked up. The mules were approaching another hairpin turn in the trail. She wouldn't be able get to whoever it was from there—and the mules couldn't back up.

Instantly she made her decision. She pulled on the mule's reins, but the animal was used to stopping only when the rest of the caravan did. He continued on. Andrea quickly dismounted anyway, climbing above the trail to let her mount pass.

"Andrea, what the hell are you doing?" Kurt shouted as his mule followed her riderless one.

"There's someone down there! We just passed him. Kurt, I think he needs help!"

Andrea heard Kurt yell to the mule-team leader to stop as she carefully backtracked along the trail. She reached the spot where she'd noticed the hiker and peered over the edge.

"Hello? Can you hear me?"

There was a movement below, then stillness.

Andrea contemplated her next move. The drop was so steep that she couldn't see anything clearly, especially with the crazy angles of the plant life on the vertical walls. She rubbed the back of her neck, frowning with indecision. Should she stay here and wait for Kurt or descend now?

"Please help me. I'm gonna fall," came a faint male voice.

Andrea's adrenaline exploded into her veins. "Kurt, I'm going down," she yelled out.

"Don't you dare! That's an order!" he shouted back, but Andrea was already off the trail, her belly to the cliff wall, her feet scrabbling for footholds. She descended toward the victim's right, making certain no loose rocks or debris would fall on him.

She was a good twenty feet below the trail when she reached the narrow ledge that held her victim. He had his back to the wall, while Andrea was facing it. She suppressed a shudder as it occurred to her that the average building ledge was probably several inches wider than this. There wasn't much between them and a half-mile drop to the Canyon floor.

"Hi. I'm Andrea," she said, taking in the pale, drained face of the man at her side. He couldn't be more than twenty years old, she guessed. "And you're off the beaten track," she said, smiling. "I'm here to correct that. What's your name?"

"Mike. And I don't feel so good."

You don't look so good, Andrea thought. She cautiously lifted his wrist to take his pulse. "What happened?"

"I was hiking up to the rim, and I got dizzy. It was so hot and . . ." His voice trailed off weakly.

"And you slipped and fell?"

Mike nodded miserably.

"Don't you worry. I've got my partner with me. Help's coming. You hang on. We'll have you out of here in no time." Andrea released his wrist, trying not to reveal her own alarm. Judging by the rapid pulse, cold, clammy skin and profuse sweating, he had a classic case of heat exhaustion. She just prayed he could remain conscious for a while longer.

"Andrea, can you hear me? Over."

Andrea reached for the radio on her belt. "I hear you, Kurt. And we've got trouble. The victim's name is Mike, he's about twenty years old—"

"Twenty-one."

"Twenty-one years old," Andrea corrected. "He's got a bad case of heat exhaustion, and his position is precarious at best." She lowered her voice. "We've got to get him out of here in a hurry, Kurt. Over."

"How secure is your footing? Over."

Andrea could feel the dirt crumbling under her feet. "We're both on shaky ground."

There was a moment's pause. Andrea looked up to see Kurt's face peering over the edge of the trail, assessing their situation.

"We've got ropes. We can haul him up with the mules," Kurt assured her. "Over."

Mike moaned, and his eyes fluttered.

"Better hurry. He's fading fast. Out."

Andrea reached for Mike's hand and squeezed it hard. "Don't pass out on me, Mike. I can't hold on to you if you fall," she said bluntly.

Mike opened his eyes.

"That's better. Why don't you tell me your name and address? Do you have any family or friends staying here at the park?" Conveying that needed information might keep him alert, Andrea decided.

It did, and she relayed the facts by radio.

"The rope's on its way down," Kurt yelled to her. He'd given up using his walkie-talkie while fixing the rope harness. "Watch for it."

Andrea lifted her head again, watching the easy progress of the harness and line down the Canyon side. She didn't try to reach for it, which would have compromised her own balance. She waited until it was right beside her before grasping it with one hand.

"Here's your ticket out, Mike," she said calmly. "I'm going to help you put this harness on. We'll go nice and slow. Take your time."

"Okay." Mike's face was paler than ever.

"Don't look down. Just look at the harness." By talking gently and moving slowly, she was able to fasten Mike in. No way could he have done the job himself, Andrea realized. "There, that wasn't so bad, was it? Now once my partner rigs a block and tackle and starts to pull you up, I want you to turn and face the wall. That way you can use your hands and feet to avoid any outcroppings."

"I will. Thanks."

Andrea gave him an encouraging smile and a thumbs-up, then keyed her radio. "He's ready when you are," she said. "Good luck, Mike. See you up top."

The mules moved forward. In jerky motions Mike started to ascend. Andrea breathed a sigh of relief as he made

steady progress back to the trail. Then she moved to where
Mike had previously stood because her section of the ledge
was weakening. Her relief vanished as the dirt crumbled
under her feet at the new location.

This ledge was unstable, too unstable to stay where she
was. She looked nervously around. She couldn't possibly
climb back up, but she *could* climb lower. There was a rocky
outcropping another ten feet below, to her right. Again the
dirt under her feet gave way, and Andrea bit her lip. It was
time to move.

She carefully maneuvered herself off the ledge and let her
feet slowly carry her down and to the right. Her hands
grabbed at the tiniest handholds. She reached the new location just as Mike reached the top of the trail. There, she
grabbed onto a bush to steady herself.

"Nice going, Kurt," she said aloud watching him and two
other men help Mike over the edge. She tipped her head
back even more to watch Mike's progress back onto the
trail. Just as she did, the ledge above her collapsed.

Rocks came flying down the Canyon wall. Andrea held
tightly onto her branch, ducked her head and closed her
eyes. Dirt flew all around, and a few of the smaller stones
bounced off her hat and shoulders. A larger stone dis-
lodged her hat altogether, and one of her arms protectively
flew to her head. In a moment, the small avalanche was
safely below her, on its way to the Colorado River.

Andrea coughed, then wiped her dusty face with a shaking hand. If she hadn't moved when she had, she'd have
fallen herself. She trembled and pressed her back flush
against the wall, forcing herself to breathe deeply.

It took a few minutes before she realized that her name
was being called, over and over again, on her radio. She
blinked at the dirt in her eyes, suddenly hearing the agonized shouts from the mule caravan above.

"Andrea ... Andrea ... Are you there, over?"

Who was that? Andrea wondered in a daze.

"Andrea, it's Kurt. Can you hear me? Come on, sweetheart, answer."

Andrea blinked again, and fumbled at her waist for the radio. That was Kurt? She barely recognized his voice, it sounded so strange.

Her own voice wasn't working so well either, she noticed. It was thin and reedy as she replied, "Claybourne here. Over."

"Andrea..." She heard her name on the radio, then a long pause. She shook her walkie-talkie, suddenly worried that the rockfall had damaged it.

"Are you there? Over?" she said, frantically keying the mike.

"Yes, I'm here. How badly are you hurt?"

Hurt? She wasn't hurt, unless you counted a few bruises on the shoulder. Suddenly she understood his worry. "Kurt, I moved to a new ledge before that one gave way."

"You moved?" His voice was incredulous.

"Yeah. I didn't like the way that ledge was crumbling. I lost my hat, but other than that, I'm fine."

"You're fine?" he echoed, doubt mingling with relief.

Andrea paused. "Well, not exactly *fine*. More like stuck. Can you get me out of here?"

"Where are you? Over."

"Look to the right of the original ledge, about fifteen feet down. There's a big bush directly above me. Over."

"What kind of bush? Over."

"How should I know?" Andrea asked heatedly. "You lectured me on geology today, not bushes." She keyed the mike off, not even bothering with an "Over." Here she'd nearly been killed, and all he could worry about was plant names.

"If you can't describe where you are, then I can't get the rope to you," he said with maddening logic. "Your botany needs work. So does your radio protocol. Now describe your location. Over."

"Trust you to find fault," Andrea complained out loud, but she made sure her mike was off first. She drew in a deep, calming breath. She'd thought her work with the airlines had made her immune to heights, but it appeared she was mistaken. Standing a half mile above the ground on a narrow ledge wasn't quite as comforting as being inside a plane.

"It's some kind of evergreen," she keyed back. "It's to the side of a jutting purple outcropping. And no, I don't know what kind of rock it is, or from what time period. Over."

"I see you now. Watch for the harness. I'll have to go to the side of the manzanita—your bush."

"Fine. So it's a manzanita," Andrea muttered. She didn't expect a pat on the back for noticing Mike's predicament, but she drew the line at being patronized. She took another look at the sheer drop beneath her feet and shuddered. "Just get me that rope."

"Do you think you can reach it? Over."

"I don't have much of a choice, do I?" she said into her radio. "I'll wave when I'm ready to be pulled up. Over and out."

Andrea hooked her walkie-talkie back to her belt. She sat back and waited for her harness. As soon as it appeared, she reached for it carefully and strapped herself in. Then she waved one arm and began the slow ascent back to the trail.

Eager hands were waiting to haul her over the edge of the trail. A smattering of applause broke out as Kurt helped her to her feet.

"How's Mike?" Andrea immediately asked when she'd finished sheding the harness and recoiling the rope.

"He's already been sent to the rim by mule. He should be close to the first-aid station by now, if he isn't there already. And that's where you're heading. Mount up."

"I'm fine," Andrea insisted, brushing off her dirty clothes. "I'd rather clean up a bit and get back to work."

"You're not going back to work." Kurt's voice lashed out with deadly intent.

Andrea looked up in surprise. "Why not?"

"Because, Ms. Claybourne, you're fired."

CHAPTER SIX

"SHE DOESN'T BELONG with the park service! I want her out of here today, Jim. I mean it."

Andrea was still reeling from the unexpected blow. Once they'd reached the South Rim, Kurt had taken her to First Aid to be checked over, then immediately reported to the personnel director's office.

"She did notice a victim you missed, Kurt," Jim said, calmly, taking in Andrea's disheveled appearance. "What did you expect her to do?"

Kurt gave Andrea a disgusted look. "I expected her to *tell* me about it, not go vaulting off her mount like the Lone Ranger."

"There wasn't enough time for that!" Andrea snapped. She remained standing, afraid of soiling Jim's office furniture with her dirty uniform. "The mules were heading for the next bend in the trail. We wouldn't have been able to backtrack!"

Kurt whirled from Jim to her. "Stopping is one thing. *Climbing* down after him without a rope is another. You're not an experienced climber! You violated every safety rule in the book!"

"He needed help right away! He looked like he was going to pass out! In fact, he nearly did!"

"You couldn't know that from the trail!" Kurt yelled. "And if he had, you couldn't have stopped him from falling unless you were anchored yourself. All you did was endanger your own life."

"I stopped him from falling! My presence kept him alert!" Andrea insisted. "And he couldn't have got into that harness himself. Jim, I swear I was in no danger."

"So you say." Kurt's eyes glittered with anger.

"So I know! You don't have the grounds to fire me! I made a perfectly valid judgment call."

"Enough, you two!" Jim ordered. "Kurt, they can hear you in the next county. Andrea, sit down—and don't worry about the upholstery. You look ready to drop."

After a baleful glance at Kurt, Andrea slumped into a chair. Kurt crossed his arms across his chest. Andrea could see that there was more than just anger on his face; there was also concern.

Jim waited a few moments, then cleared his throat. "You spotted the young man when no one else did, Andrea. You made your decision to go after him, and the end results were successful. In view of those facts, I don't think any further action is warranted."

Andrea exhaled a slow sigh of relief. "Thank you."

Kurt started to speak, but Jim held up a hand, effectively cutting him off.

"Kurt, is there a chance that you're being overprotective?"

"Overprotective?" he repeated incredulously. "How would you suggest I react when my rookie jumps off her mule and throws herself over the edge of the trail? Andrea lacks common sense!"

"I don't think so," Jim countered. "I do think you're afraid to trust Andrea—or any other rookie, for that matter. I know it's been hard for you since Sarah died."

"This has nothing to do with Sarah!"

"Doesn't it?" Jim asked quietly.

Andrea suddenly remembered Kurt's earlier words to her. *I don't want you to end up like Sarah Wolf.*

"No, it doesn't." Kurt gave first Jim, then Andrea, a look of rage. "But since you insist on bringing up my wife's name, I will say this. When Sarah was my rookie, she followed my orders to the letter. *Not* like Andrea Claybourne. I won't be responsible for her safety any longer."

Andrea felt her heart painfully skip a beat. Kurt didn't want her as a partner anymore? Her face must have shown her distress, because Jim gave her a reassuring smile.

"Andrea, why don't you take the rest of the day off?"

"But..."

"Go get yourself cleaned up while Kurt and I talk this thing through. I'll see you here tomorrow morning at eight."

Andrea rose wearily to her feet.

"And Andrea?"

"Yes, Jim?"

"Good job."

She gave Jim a halfhearted smile that quickly disappeared at Kurt's open disapproval.

Andrea walked back to the ranger quarters with a heavy heart. She'd only tried to help a fellow human being in trouble, and all it had gotten her was more trouble. Andrea lifted her chin, reflecting that, despite everything, she'd do it over again in a second. Sometimes you couldn't sit around and analyze everything—you just had to act. The plane crash had taught her that.

She trudged through the slow moving, snarled tourist traffic of Grand Canyon Village to the rangers' brown wood building. A hot bath in her quarters would feel good, she thought, rubbing a particularly sore spot on her shoulder.

That, and some aspirin. Her head was starting to ache with the stress of the day. Or rather, she told herself, the stress of being around Kurt Marlowe.

A half hour later, she stepped out of the tub. She was cleaner, but she definitely didn't feel much better. Her back ached from the mule ride; muscles long unused were vehemently making their protests known. Her headache had settled into a persistent pounding despite the aspirin, and her left shoulder was turning a mottled purple.

Andrea dried and combed out her hair, then threw on a pair of denim shorts and a striped tank top. With ice from the hall soda machine, she applied a pack to her shoulder. That must have been some rock, she thought, lifting the ice to study the welt. Thank goodness it hadn't hit her head.

She shivered at the thought, slapped the ice pack down, and sat cross-legged on the bed. She'd have to buy a new hat before she went back on the trail. Any needed uniform replacements had to come out of her own pocket. She'd been given her free issue of uniforms when first hired, and she wouldn't get any more until the anniversary date of her hiring. Perhaps later she'd go out for the hat. Maybe she'd even try one of the village's restaurants instead of eating in the chow hall. Anything to distract her from thoughts of Kurt Marlowe.

Andrea faced the truth. Deep down, she didn't want to lose him as a partner, and that surprised her. She'd come to Arizona to start her life afresh. While she hadn't ruled out forming new attachments, she certainly hadn't expected any possibilities to appear quite so soon. It was rather unsettling.

Yet the feelings inside her couldn't be denied. There was something about Kurt that Andrea couldn't help but admire. He was his own person, and he spoke his own mind. All his actions stemmed from a respect for life. And his energy, his vigor, made him seem bigger than life, somehow.

All in all, he was such a refreshing change from the other men she'd known that she found it harder and harder to resist his attraction.

Andrea sighed. She felt nauseated, her head still hurt and her shoulder throbbed. She readjusted the ice pack. Between her discomfort and the pain of Kurt's desertion, any appetite for dinner was gone. She wondered whom she'd get as a replacement. Probably someone dull like Dan, she thought ruefully. Kurt might be a lot of things, but he was never, ever dull.

A knock on the door startled her.

"Come in," she called out. "It's not locked."

The door opened, and Andrea found herself looking up at Kurt. She felt her pulse quicken with excitement, then compensated by giving him a less-than-enthusiastic welcome.

"Well, this is a surprise. I didn't expect to see my partner again today. Or is it ex-partner?"

Kurt closed the door behind him. "Jim wanted me to stop by."

She should have known it wasn't his own idea, she thought bitterly. But all she said was, "You didn't answer my question."

"That's why I'm here. Jim left that decision up to us." Kurt crossed over to her bed and reached for the ice pack. "Let me see that."

"It's nothing," she said, pulling away from him, but he took the ice pack from her hand just the same.

He studied her purple shoulder, frowning. "That's one hell of a bruise."

"Falling rocks tend to have that effect," Andrea replied flippantly. "May I have my ice?"

Kurt replaced the pack on her shoulder with a gentleness that couldn't help but affect her. "Did you take some aspirin?"

"Yes." Andrea felt his fingers brush against hers as she reanchored the pack, and again experienced that sense of heightened awareness she always noticed in his presence. "Kurt, I really don't feel like company."

"I'm not leaving until we talk. Jim's waiting for our decision." Kurt sat down next to her on the bed.

Andrea hardened her heart. "Well, the way I figure it, I've made it through almost half of my probation with you. If I can do that, I can make it through another thirty days with *anyone*."

Andrea saw Kurt start at her words, but somehow that gave her no satisfaction. She fussed with the pack, avoiding his gaze.

"Jim can find me someone else tomorrow morning. That's what you want, isn't it?"

"I want to hear what *you* want, Andrea," Kurt said with a strange, unreadable expression.

"I just told you. I want a new partner. Why should I keep working with someone who doesn't trust me? All I'll ever be to you is a stupid stewardess who can't make the grade."

"I don't believe that, Andrea. I haven't for quite some time. But that doesn't mean I don't worry about you."

Andrea gave him a look of disbelief, but said nothing.

"If that rock had hit your head instead of your shoulder, I'd be sending your parents a telegram right now asking about funeral arrangements."

Andrea clenched her fingers at his bluntness. "And if I hadn't done what I did, you'd be sending Mike's family one instead."

"I know."

"You—you admit it?"

"Yes. I should have congratulated you on the rescue, not tried to fire you. Jim was right. I am being overprotective. It won't happen again." His eyes caught hers as she finally lifted her head. "I'd like to finish your training, if that's okay with you."

Andrea couldn't believe it. This was what she'd waited so long to hear. Yet proving Kurt wrong didn't fill her with triumph. Instead, she found herself admiring his integrity—and questioning her own motives. The memory of his warm body against hers, his mouth touching hers, flashed into her mind. It was becoming harder and harder for Andrea to concentrate on her job.

She took in a deep breath, and made up her mind. "I don't think that's a good idea. I'd rather you called Jim and asked for a new rookie."

Andrea saw Kurt's shoulders tense. For a moment there was an awful silence in the room.

"I didn't think you were a quitter, Andrea Claybourne. Was I wrong?"

"I—" She knew Kurt wanted her to stay on as his partner. But did she dare? Because suddenly she knew what she wanted. She wanted Kurt Marlowe to be aware of her as a woman, not just another rookie. Only that wasn't going to happen if she ruined her probation by concentrating on him instead of her job.

"It isn't too late to change your mind," Kurt said.

"That's what I'm afraid of," Andrea murmured, more to herself than to him.

Kurt's lips drew together in a thin line. "Jim said that if he didn't hear from us by morning he'd leave us together. If you want a new partner, *you* make the call." He stiffly rose from the bed. "I won't."

Andrea watched him leave. With a heavy heart, she forced herself to pick up the phone. She had more sense than to get involved with a man still obsessed with his late wife—especially while she was still on probation.

Reluctantly she punched in the personnel office extension. Jim himself answered on the third ring.

"I've been expecting your call, Andrea," he said after inquiring about her condition. "What have you decided?"

"Jim, I—" Andrea stopped, unable to bring herself to say the words just yet. "I'm so confused. Why didn't anyone tell me Sarah was Kurt's wife? Why didn't *you*?"

"I keep my employees' personal and professional lives separate," Jim said bluntly. "That applies to everyone."

"It shouldn't, not when Kurt's personal life directly affects my professional status," Andrea argued. "I deserve to know what's going on. Sarah's death was two years ago, and so was the investigation. Yet Kurt still acts like there's some sort of cover-up. He disappears mysteriously on weekends and . . . and no one tells me anything!"

Silence on the other line.

"Jim, I feel like I'm being kept in the dark. Is there anything else I should know?"

"Nothing," Jim said firmly, but Andrea had the distinct impression that he wasn't telling all. "This conversation is taking up valuable time. Unless you request otherwise, *right now,* you and Kurt will continue working together."

"But—"

"Goodbye, Andrea."

Jim hung up, leaving Andrea with more questions than answers. She should call him right back to request a new instructor. But she couldn't seem to do it. *Later,* Andrea promised as she quickly hung up. *I'll call later.* She didn't. Instead, she delayed her decision for so long that the events of the day finally caught up with her and she fell into a deep, dreamless sleep. She woke up a few hours later to the sound of repeated knocking.

Still groggy, she stumbled to the door.

It was a deliveryman. "Are you Andrea Claybourne?"

"Yes, that's me."

"Package. Sign here."

Andrea quickly did so. "Let me get my purse," she mumbled.

"No need. The tip's all taken care of." The man handed her a sealed bag. "Enjoy."

"Thank you." she closed the door, then sat down on her bed and opened the package. All thoughts of calling Jim vanished as she saw the contents.

Inside was a brand-new ranger hat.

THE HAT WAS THE ONLY concession Andrea allowed Kurt to make. The next week she stayed strictly within the bounds of her role as rookie ranger. She allowed no personal conversation, no everyday intimacies as Kurt took her through the safety procedures used in rope rescues.

Andrea learned to climb up cliffs, then rappel down. The physical strain was nothing compared to the mental concentration required, and Andrea found herself collapsing wherever she bedded down for the night. But before her eyes closed in sheer exhaustion, she congratulated herself on surviving yet another day of hiding her attraction to Kurt Marlowe. So far she'd passed all his tests with flying colors. She'd kept their relationship on a simple business footing, at least on the surface.

Andrea consoled herself with the thought that maybe she and Kurt could become friends once she'd finished her probation. Perhaps even more than friends . . . After all, Sarah had been dead two years. He might be ready for someone new in his life, someone like her. Until her probation was safely up, though, Andrea had intention of risking her job by romantically pursuing her instructor.

Unless, Andrea thought hopefully, unless he showed some sign of interest in her. Unfortunately, the only romantic interest anyone professed came from Dan.

"Come on, Andrea, you and I could have a lot of fun," he pleaded after one of her rappelling sessions. "Go out with me."

"I've told you before, Dan. No, thank you," Andrea said in her coolest, most dismissive voice.

Dan's face turned ugly. "Don't hold your breath waiting for the high-and-mighty Kurt Marlowe to ask you out. I've seen the way you look at him," he said slyly. "Well, let me tell you, no one's good enough for his daughter, not even a—"

"His daughter?" Andrea was flabbergasted. "Kurt has a *daughter?*"

But Dan was more concerned with his bruised ego than with explanations. "Don't come running to me when you get lonely. There's plenty of other fish in the sea."

Despite her curiosity about Kurt's child, Andrea refused to have anything more to do with Dan. But his revelation upset her more than she cared to admit. It was hard enough competing with Sarah for Kurt's attention. But she couldn't in good conscience compete with a child. No wonder she never saw Kurt on weekends. He must be with his daughter.

Andrea went back to her training with a heavy heart, but by the end of the week she was able to accomplish any task he set her. The rappelling lessons finally ended with a particularly brutal exam. Frequent rests were needed during the rappel downward; during one break, Andrea lifted a hand to fuss with her hair, which had started to work free from its braid.

Kurt frowned, but Andrea continued to pat a few loose strands back into place.

"We're a quarter mile above the river. If you lose your grip, it's a long way down."

"I'm not about to fall," she argued, but replaced her hand on the rope. Her body swayed slightly at the action.

"There's a time for everything, and rappelling isn't an appropriate time for primping." Kurt studied her carefully. "I know you're not stupid. I'm inclined to believe you're deliberately trying to annoy me."

Andrea's answer was a guilty silence. She *was* giving him a hard time, but only because she wanted to keep a distance between them. Annoying him was one way to avoid any disturbing closeness and to hide her growing attraction. It also prevented her from asking any personal, curious, unwarranted questions.

Did Kurt really have a daughter? And why had he never mentioned her?

"You had your chance to get another instructor, Andrea. Since you didn't take advantage of it, I suggest a rapid improvement in your behavior."

Andrea felt her cheeks flush with guilt. This time when Kurt gave the order to start descending again, Andrea's easy progress didn't disguise her concentration and attention to safety. Kurt touched the bottom first and watched her reach the Canyon floor.

"Congratulations. You've passed this section of your probation."

"Thank you," she breathed with relief. She would be glad of a break. Rappelling was hard on the body. The old bruise on her shoulder had several fresh ones elsewhere to keep it company.

"Now get your gear. We're going to catch a mule ride to the top."

"And then?"

"Then we pack for tomorrow. It's time for the next phase of your training. We'll be heading down the Colorado."

"We're going to hike some new trails?"

"No, we're going white-river rafting," he corrected. "Tomorrow morning we'll catch a flight to Lees Ferry at the Arizona-Utah border, and start the trip there. If the weather stays good, we'll raft all the way to Pearce Ferry."

Andrea recalled that Pearce Ferry was near Nevada, at the far western border of the park. "You mean we'll be traveling down the entire length of the Canyon?"

"Yes." Kurt began to coil up his ropes and motioned for Andrea to do the same. "You don't seem very excited," he observed.

"I'm just a little nervous." That was the understatement of the year. The water didn't frighten her, but the possibility of being alone in a raft with Kurt did. "Who's going with us?"

"No one."

Andrea felt her heart skip a beat. "You mean..."

"That's right, Ms. Claybourne. It'll be just the two of us."

"ARE YOU ALL RIGHT?"

Andrea started at the sound of Kurt's voice. "Of course. Why?"

"Because our plane hasn't even left the ground, and you're white-knuckling the armrests."

"I am not," Andrea denied, immediately releasing her death grip on the seat. She carefully folded her hands in her lap. "I'm just fine."

Andrea took in a deep breath, forcing herself to do the calm breathing her airline counselor had taught her. If only she were anywhere else but on this plane! She'd give her life's savings to simply disappear for the next ten minutes. Takeoffs were the worst. It was during takeoff that her plane had abruptly dropped like a rock in a pond. Andrea gulped in another breath, and tried not to remember how the big plane had torn into two ugly pieces. A small plane like this would probably break into many more....

Andrea trembled.

Kurt gave her an appraising look, but she turned away from his scrutiny and stared out the window. They were at Grand Canyon Airport, waiting for their light plane to fly them to Lees Ferry.

Late last night Andrea had finished packing. But the excitement of the raft trip had given way to anxiety when she'd received her plane ticket from the ranger office early this morning. That anxiety had grown worse when her gear was loaded, her seat belt fastened, and she had to wait for take-off.

Kurt frowned. "You don't look all right," he said. "Listen, if you're feeling ill, we can get off and make a later flight."

"And give you a chance to tell Jim I get airsick? Which I don't, by the way. Jim wants me to fly with the helicopters full-time after my probation's over. The last thing I need is for you to start trouble."

Thank goodness helicopter lift-offs were nothing like airplane takeoffs.

"I wouldn't do that," Kurt replied calmly.

Andrea was agitated, but she couldn't fail to notice the sincerity in his voice. "Of course you wouldn't. Sorry. I'll be fine." Her brave words faltered when the plane's engine revved up. She bit her lip as they began to taxi, concentrating once more on her breathing exercises. They didn't help. She gripped the armrests again as the plane's speed increased, and forced herself to keep her eyes open.

Suddenly she felt Kurt take her near hand between both of his and hold it tightly. She almost pulled away, but then she let her fingers curl around his and held on for dear life as the plane took off. Andrea cringed, swallowing hard as the wheels thumped and were retracted.

Her breathing exercises—or was it his reassuring presence?—helped greatly. She felt her shivering subside, and gradually the plane leveled out. Andrea gave a great sigh, then saw that Kurt's eyes were focused intently on her.

"Go ahead and say it," she said, waiting for the inevitable.

"Say what?"

"For an ex-flight attendant, I'm awfully nervous about flying." Embarrassed, she tried to pull her hand away, but Kurt held it firmly within his grasp.

"I'm sure you're used to much bigger planes. These small propeller jobs can make even veteran fliers nervous," he said kindly.

"This is the first little one I've ever been in," she admitted.

"There you go. You're also used to taking off on proper runways, not minute strips built for tourist flights. I was tense the first time I flew here, too."

"Really?"

"Sure. But you get used to it. I did." Kurt gave her a careful once-over. "Are you all right now?"

"Yes, thank you." She smiled at him with gratitude. Kurt hadn't known how upset she still felt during takeoffs. He couldn't imagine how his kind words had helped, how touched she was by his concern. "I'm fine. Fine enough, in fact, to discuss finances. You bought me a new hat when I lost my other one. What do I owe you?"

"Nothing."

Andrea made a scoffing sound. "You expect me to believe replacement hats come free?"

"No, I expect you to believe that I hate waiting around uniform stores. Spare me from women on shopping expeditions." He rolled his eyes, but Andrea saw the mirth in them.

"Very funny," she said, enjoying the camaraderie she'd craved so much. "But please let me pay you back."

Kurt waved her off. "Later. I want to relax right now. We have a strenuous week ahead of us." He settled back in his seat and closed his eyes.

Andrea hid a smile. Somehow she knew he'd never take the money she owed him. Beneath the gruff exterior was a generous soul. As she studied Kurt in repose, she wondered what other qualities were hidden inside.

He must have felt her gaze, because he opened his eyes. "Can't you rest? We can change seats if you want," he suggested. "Maybe you'll be more comfortable away from the window."

Andrea looked outside at the riot of colors beneath her and shook her head. "I never get tired of looking at the Canyon. But thanks for offering."

Kurt nodded. "The scenery is fantastic. Too bad it's such a short flight."

"I'll get a longer aerial view when I start training with the helicopters."

"You'll like it. Everyone does."

"I won't have any problems," Andrea assured him. "But what about you?"

"Me?"

"Our trip is bound to bring back memories of Sarah," she said softly. "Will you be all right?"

For a minute she thought Kurt wasn't going to answer.

Then, "I never look forward to rafting past the location where she died. I was on flight duty when they found her. I had to fly her out, you know," he said in a bleak, colorless voice.

"No, I didn't." Andrea was shocked; instinctively she laid a comforting hand on his arm.

"We had a lot of snow two winters ago, and the spring runoff was high. The rapids were especially dangerous, the currents even faster than they normally are. The boaters drowned at a steep drop in the river. Everyone said it was a miracle we even found them—and Sarah" His voice was harsh with emotion.

"You don't believe in miracles?" Andrea asked quietly, almost to herself.

"I don't believe Sarah should have died at all!"

A few curious heads turned their way, and Kurt compressed his lips into a thin line. Andrea waited until the other passengers went back to their business, then said, "Kurt, I'm sorry, but I don't understand."

Kurt exhaled slowly. "I trained Sarah myself, Andrea. Not that she needed much training. She was good—one of the best I've ever seen! Her death was no accident."

Cold shivers snaked down Andrea's spine.

"Something went wrong on that rescue, something that wasn't her fault. I would have trusted Sarah with my own life, she was that good. And her equipment was top-notch."

"Are you saying Sarah's death was the result of someone else's error?" Andrea was incredulous. "Some other staff member?"

"I'm saying Sarah's dead, and she shouldn't be."

Andrea felt her heart ache with compassion. "You can't blame others, Kurt. It's not right—or healthy," she said gently.

"You think it's only grief talking?" His eyes denied the accusation, but Andrea had to be honest.

"I think it's a possibility. I'm sure anything questionable would surely have come out at the official inquiry."

Kurt gave her a skeptical look.

"Did you suspect anything two years ago?" Andrea asked.

"I didn't know what to think. The other staff involved in that ill-fated rescue barely talked about it, at least to me. Sarah's own partner asked to be transferred to an obscure section of the Canyon."

"They had to be upset, like you were," Andrea replied.

"Maybe."

"And Kurt, that hearing was two years ago. Why this obsession with Sarah's death now?"

"Because of you."

"*Me?*"

"Yes. I didn't want you working here, and Sarah was part of the reasoning. Then, all of sudden, everyone clammed up again at Sarah's name." Kurt's face was morose. "Think about it, Andrea. Jim won't talk about her. Sarah's old

partners won't either. No one's saying a word. Any workplace has gossip, yet you yourself hadn't even heard that
Sarah was my wife!''

Or that you had a child, Andrea thought to herself. "The
subject of you and Sarah does seem to be off-limits," Andrea agreed. She'd wondered about this earlier and still
found it surprising that, except for Dan's venomous remark, she'd heard barely any mention of Kurt and no mention at all of Sarah or the accident.

"Still off-limits after two whole years? Doesn't that strike
you as suspicious?"

Andrea held out her hands in confusion. "Maybe they're
avoiding the subject because they're uncomfortable. Maybe
they want to spare you pain."

"Hiding the truth from me won't accomplish that. No
matter how long it takes, I won't rest until I find out what
really happened."

The remainder of the flight was made in silence.

Andrea was aware that Kurt was watching her closely as
the plane began to descend, but she was nervous only during takeoffs. Landings didn't bother her. After a few moments of scrutiny, Kurt returned to his own reflections.

She wished she could help. It was bad enough that Sarah
was dead, but much worse that he thought her death pre-
ventable. As terrible as the loss of Dee had been, at least
Andrea wasn't tortured with thoughts of what might have
been. Dee's death was unavoidable. But what about Kurt's
wife?

Were Kurt's accusations merely grief-induced? Or worse
yet, was there an element of truth in his assumptions? Either way, Andrea now knew why Kurt worried about her. A
woman like Sarah, with military and fire-department experience as well as Kurt's training, had died on the job. Kurt
had to be wondering what kind of chance Andrea Claybourne stood.

Strangely enough, Andrea wasn't worried about her own abilities. But she *was* worried about Kurt. She knew better than anyone how the past could come back to haunt you. Then and there, Andrea vowed to find out exactly how Sarah Wolf had died. She didn't want Kurt unhappy, nor did she want Sarah continually in his thoughts.

Kurt's peace of mind depended on it. And no matter how Andrea tried to deny it, so did her own.

CHAPTER SEVEN

"I'LL TAKE CARE of the raft. Why don't you change?" Kurt suggested.

Andrea nodded. They were at the base of Glen Canyon Dam just below Lake Powell. The Colorado River stretched before them, its surface deceptively calm, giving no indication of the powerful current below. Kurt unpacked the raft and inflated it with a portable foot pump while Andrea shed her uniform and boots to expose the red ranger's bathing suit underneath. She put her boots and clothes away in a waterproof bag.

She then slipped a pair of old canvas sneakers onto her bare feet and watched as Kurt set the oars in their locks. "We won't be using a motor?" she asked curiously.

Kurt shook his head. "No. Motorized rafts are from twenty to thirty feet long and need six to fifteen people for balance. We don't have enough weight for one."

He started loading his gear, and Andrea did the same.

"Our four-man raft will hold us and our supplies just fine. As long as we use the oars for steering, the current will take us downriver. I hope you know how to paddle."

"I do, but I'm out of practice."

"We'll take it easy, then, so you don't end up with sore shoulders."

"Don't worry about me."

Kurt gave her an appraising look. "I'm beginning to see why Jim hired you. You thrive on challenges."

And Kurt was the biggest challenge of all. But she couldn't say that, so she busied herself with unpacking her sun block and life jacket. She was just buckling on the vest when another ranger approached. Both she and Kurt glanced up expectantly.

"Yes, Earl?" Kurt asked the man, with whom Andrea was unfamiliar.

"My partner and I caught a flight up this morning. We're heading downriver, too. I noticed you two hadn't picked up your mail, Kurt, so I grabbed it for you."

"Why, thank you," Andrea said gratefully. She took the bundle of letters he passed her. Her parents and friends were faithful writers, and she was always happy to get news of home. "I'm Andrea Claybourne, by the way," she said, holding out her hand.

"Earl Delmont." The other ranger gave her an amiable shake of the hand before turning to Kurt. "You could have picked up your mail at Phantom Ranch later when you stopped for supplies, but I thought you might like it now."

"Appreciate it, Earl," Kurt said.

Earl paused, then asked, "How are you, Kurt?"

"Just fine."

Earl nodded. "Nice meeting you, Andrea, but I've got to be going. Have a safe trip down the river."

"Thanks—you, too. And thank you for the mail." Andrea waited until Earl was out of earshot, then said, "It was awfully kind of him to make the extra trip with our mail."

"It wasn't kindness that brought Earl out here. It was his mother-hen instinct."

"What?"

"Earl was part of the team that assisted Sarah and her partner during that water rescue," Kurt explained. "He's been checking up on me for the past two years."

Andrea's shocked gaze followed the man who'd just left. Kurt calmly finished packing the gear.

"Along with Sarah's old partner and Earl's present one, he's one of the three who keeps insisting those four deaths were an unfortunate *accident*." Kurt's lip gave an ironic twist. "That word covers a multitude of sins."

"You think he's lying?" Andrea asked bluntly.

"Not lying. Just not telling everything."

"How can you act so...so composed in his presence?"

Kurt shrugged. "Earl's heart's in the right place. Besides, anger won't solve the problem. Sooner or later I'll find out what really happened."

"Have you talked to Jim lately?"

"Yeah, I have. I've also reviewed the reports filed by the other three rangers. Not much new there. They're the same ones I read two years ago. Jim assured me he's satisfied with the original finding of accidental death."

"But you aren't."

"No, I'm not." Kurt put on his life jacket, then checked to make sure all the supplies were tied down properly. He waved Andrea away when she would have helped.

Andrea didn't protest, but quietly stowed their mail. In less than a minute, they were on the river and under way. The Canyon walls rose above them in a majestic array of purples and beiges. Their varied faces, ledges and planes served to isolate the river and its occupants from the outside world. Andrea welcomed the tranquillity. Her rhythmic rowing and the gentle rocking motion of the raft had a calming effect.

Kurt must have experienced the same. After a while he spoke again, his voice easily heard above the waters.

"I shouldn't have upset you with my problems."

Andrea ceased her paddling. "I'm not upset. But I am concerned about you."

"Why?"

"Because it's so important to you to prove everyone else wrong. It's been two years, Kurt. It's time to get on with your life. Wouldn't it be easier to let matters rest?"

"Perhaps, but I can't."

You mean you won't, Andrea silently corrected.

"You must miss Sarah very much," she said with quiet envy.

Kurt also stopped paddling and turned to face her. "I do. She was stubborn, hot-tempered and prone to argue about everything—like me." He shrugged, smiling a little. "She was a very important part of my life. I'm glad we decided to have a child before she died."

"So you do have a child," she murmured. Andrea felt another pang of envy, this one stronger than before. She'd always enjoyed being around children, but what she felt now was more than that. For the first time in her life, Andrea yearned to have a child of her own.

She was suddenly glad Kurt had something left after the tragedy that had ended his marriage.

"A daughter. Lynn's five now." Kurt looked at her sharply. "You heard?"

"One of the few pieces of gossip I did hear." Andrea thought of Dan. "Considering the source, however, I wasn't certain."

"Why didn't you ask me?"

"I didn't want to pry." Andrea smiled. "Lynn's a pretty name. Where is she? In Flagstaff?" That was the city closest to the Grand Canyon.

"Not anymore. Sarah and I used to lived there, but my parents in Phoenix took Lynn when Sarah died. I go home every weekend to see her."

Andrea thought of her own weekends spent with no family, no children, no Kurt—just casual friends and idle conversation. Suddenly she felt more alone than ever.

"I thought about moving Lynn back to Flagstaff, but she seems happy with my parents," Kurt was saying.

"And that's why you're considering a new job with the environmental protection group in Phoenix?" Andrea asked with sudden insight. "Because of Lynn?"

Kurt nodded. "My parents were a big help to me. With this job, I couldn't have taken care of a three-year old. But Lynn's not a baby anymore, and my parents are getting on in years. I need to be a bigger part of Lynn's life. She starts school this September. If I joined the agency, I could arrange my work to coincide with her school hours."

Andrea felt an almost physical ache at the thought of Kurt moving so far away. "Won't you hate working indoors?"

"Giving up my job is a small price to pay. My parents need a rest, and I miss my daughter. I never planned that Lynn and I would be separated for so long. But I want to find out what happened to Sarah before I quit."

The raft began to slide sideways in the gentle current, and this time it was Andrea who made the course correction with her oars.

"You may never find out," she pointed out. "September's only three months away."

"I have to find out, Andrea! Sarah had so much to live for! She was full of plans for us and for Lynn, and to lose it all like she did—" His voice grew harsh. "I owe it to Sarah to find out who was responsible."

"And if no one was, Kurt? What then?"

"Someone *has* to be at fault. It wasn't Sarah. I know, I supervised her probation. Whoever was responsible for Sarah's death doesn't belong with the park service. I want them fired, then I want Lynn to know her mother wasn't the helpless drowning victim people think she was. There's not much else I can do for Sarah now, but I *can* salvage her reputation."

"And that's important to you?"

"It's for Lynn, too. And I know it would matter to Sarah. She took great pride in her work."

"You may never know for certain," Andrea said again. "It's been a long time, Kurt."

"That's right, it has, and everyone's still touchy every time her name is mentioned. Sarah's death was no accident," he said fiercely. "At least, no accident that *she* caused."

Andrea's eyes were sad. "But as long as you don't leave room in your heart for that possibility, you'll never be able to let her go."

Kurt abruptly turned around and began to paddle. After a few moments, Andrea joined in with her oars. She wanted to talk to him about Dee, to tell him how hard it had been to let her own friend go. But once you did, she wanted to explain to him, your life became easier, not harder. The living had to go on living—in the present, not the past. But Kurt had made it clear that he was in no frame of mind for more conversation. Andrea decided she'd try again later.

Right now she had her own emotions to deal with. She couldn't in all honesty deny the sudden despair she'd felt when Kurt told her he was leaving in the fall. The intensity of her feelings was a revelation. Being far away from friends and family was bad enough; Andrea couldn't deny that she was lonely at times. But Kurt had brought an excitement to her life she knew she'd miss.

Andrea respected his abilities, his dedication. And she admired his loyalty to his daughter and to the memory of his wife. She couldn't disregard him as a ranger, and she certainly couldn't disregard him as a man. But she couldn't compete with a ghost.... Andrea vowed anew to help discover how Kurt's wife had really died. Only then would he be free to care for someone else. Only then would she have the right to explore her own feelings for him.

The sun rose higher and grew hotter, and the current started to flow faster. By noon Andrea's shoulders were sore from paddling. It was a welcome relief to hear Kurt announce that they were stopping for the day as soon as he spotted a suitable place to camp.

"Even the commercial rafting trips only stay on the river half a day," he remarked as they paddled toward shore. "It gets dark quickly in the Canyon, even in summer. It isn't smart to be on the Colorado then. Besides, I imagine your arms need a rest."

"I'm more interested in just standing up and moving around." Andrea looked with eager eyes toward the bank. "Sitting all morning in this raft tires me out more than hiking the trails."

"You can hike after we eat and set up camp," Kurt told her. "There are lots of side canyons and Indian ruins that aren't accessible from anyplace except the river. If you feel like exploring, I'd be happy to show you around."

"I'd like that," Andrea said eagerly. "I even brought along my camera this time."

It was packed away in the airtight ammunition containers that all rafters used. Kurt had explained that they were the most inexpensive, effective way to protect valuables against the crushing power of the rapids.

"I'd love to get some pictures of the wildlife, too," she said. Forcing herself to appear casual, she added, "Speaking of wildlife, whatever happened to the burro we choppered out?"

"The last I heard, she was doing quite well, considering."

"She's still alive?" Andrea was amazed. "They didn't put her down?"

Kurt threw her an exasperated look. "I told you I'd have the pilot put in a good word with the vet. It looks as if the foal will have a full recovery, and get adopted out."

Andrea exhaled with relief. "I'm so glad. Thanks, Kurt."

"For what? The baby was healthy. I had nothing to do with it. Now if you still want to stretch your legs, we'd better get lunch started."

But soon after they'd eaten, the sky darkened as massive black clouds moved in. She and Kurt barely managed to repack the food and set up their tents before the rain began to fall in earnest. Andrea found herself sitting inside on her sleeping bag, staring out at the rain with disappointment.

"Can I come in?" Kurt called through the partially closed tent flap.

"Of course. Hurry up, you'll get wet."

Kurt crawled into her tent with Andrea's bathing suit and towel in hand. Andrea had changed into shorts and shirt, as had Kurt.

"You left these out on the clothesline. They're still damp, but maybe they'll dry in here."

"Thanks." She took them from him. "Wait," she said as he started to leave. "I still have your mail, remember?" Andrea reached inside the waterproof clothes bag where she'd stowed it earlier. "Maybe if we're lucky we'll each get a nice long letter instead of a bunch of bills."

"My parents don't write much since I'm home most weekends, but Lynn surprises me from time to time. I taught her to print the alphabet, and Mom helps her out." Kurt sat cross-legged on the ground cloth. "I wouldn't mind a letter from Lynn right now. It doesn't look as if we're going anywhere."

"No, it doesn't. Why don't you have some coffee while I separate your mail from mine?" She passed him the coffeepot and a cup. "I brought it inside when the rain started. It shouldn't be too cold. That's why my swimsuit was still outside. I have my priorities." She smiled.

Kurt's face brightened. "You're a camper after my own heart." He took off his rain slicker, then poured himself a cup.

"Here you go." Andrea gave him his mail, then flipped through hers. "Bill, advertisement, car insurance... Hey, I'm in luck. Here's a letter from my parents, and it looks like—" She broke off as the block printing on the next envelope caught her eye. It was from Emily.

Kurt lifted his head from his own mail. "Not another bill, I hope?"

"No, no... Just a letter from a little girl I met back in Denver. I heard from her last week. I'm surprised she's writing again so soon." Andrea tossed the rest of her mail on the ground. "Will you think me terribly rude if I read this while you finish your coffee?"

"Not at all," Kurt said. "I have one here from an old college friend, so I'll see what he has to say."

Andrea nodded and eagerly slit open the envelope from Emily. Her letters usually came with a separate hand-drawn picture in bright colors, but there was no such picture this time. Instead, Emily's short note of greeting was accompanied by a letter in adult handwriting.

Andrea read it first.

Dear Miss Claybourne,
My wife and I are taking Emily on her long-awaited vacation to visit her grandparents and see the Grand Canyon. The five of us are most eager to see you again and to thank you in person. Emily wouldn't be alive today if it wasn't for your efforts.

The letter concluded with dates and travel arrangements, a hotel phone number, and a request for Andrea to contact them as soon as possible. Andrea noted that Emily's family should be arriving in the Canyon at about the halfway point of her rafting trip. She could call them from Phantom Ranch. It would take three days before she and Kurt reached it, but that posed no problem. The family planned on staying at the Canyon for a week.

Andrea then read Emily's letter.

Dear Andrea,
I'm so happy! I finally get to see my grandparents and you.

And was underlined three times, Andrea saw with amusement.

Do you like your new job better than your old one? Will you let me take a picture of you? Dad says I can borrow his camera. I can't wait. See you soon!
                                              Love, Emily

P.S. The doctor says my leg is all better now.

Andrea smiled. She'd enjoy seeing Emily again. She'd met her parents in the hospital and had seen photos of the grandparents. It was almost as though she was now an honorary member of the family.

"Good news?" Kurt asked.

Andrea realized she was still smiling. "Yes. Some people I know from Denver are coming to visit me. It'll be good to see familiar faces."

Kurt slanted her an inquisitive look. "Would one of these friends happen to be a single male?"

"I beg your pardon?"

"You don't have to answer that," Kurt said immediately. "It's none of my business."

A pleased Andrea couldn't resist commenting on his interest. Perhaps Sarah didn't occupy his thoughts *all* the time. She folded the letter and placed it inside its envelope.

"That's an awfully leading question," she said lightly. "You should have started out with something tamer, like what's my favorite food or where did I go to school?"

"What's your favorite food?"

"Chocolate." She grinned. "Not very original, I'm afraid, but there it is."

"A popular choice. Not too many people could fault you on it."

"No." Andrea shifted on her sleeping bag, listening to the rain, which was coming down even harder.

Kurt zipped the tent flap all the way shut, then settled himself more comfortably.

"So where did you go to school?" he asked.

"Denver, of course. I went through the grades with the same people year after year. My parents were born there, too, and they've lived in one house all their married life."

"Did you have a steady sweetheart in high school?"

"Me?" Andrea shook her head. "No. I was a thin, gawky teenager who was taller than all the boys in class. I never managed to find my own dates."

"That's hard to believe," Kurt said with an appreciative glimmer in his eye.

"Oh, it's true. I was an extremely late bloomer. All the Claybourne women are. But I was lucky. Dee—" Andrea stopped abruptly, then started again. "Dee was very popular. She always used to fix me up on double dates. The boys were so crazy about Dee that they'd date me just to be near her."

Andrea was silent, thinking of Dee and herself as teenagers. Dee was all giggles and fun, and determined that the more serious Andrea would share in that lightheartedness.

"Dee was a friend?"

"Yes. My best friend," Andrea said softly. "We were like sisters. I was an only child, and Dee had two brothers. We lived next door to each other. She was always there for me. Mom said we started playing together when we were in diapers." Her voice was choked. "Dee died in an accident a few months ago."

To her horror she felt her eyes fill with tears that spilled onto her face. Kurt made a sound of dismay, then gathered her into his lap. With one hand he reached into his jeans pocket and pulled out a clean bandanna. He passed it to her, and Andrea swiped at her cheeks.

For a while there was no sound except the steady beating rain outside the tent and Andrea's painful sobbing. She felt Kurt's hand stoke her back, and took comfort from his touch.

"I'm sorry," she said when she finally got control of herself. "I didn't mean to fall apart like that. Sometimes it just...sneaks up on me."

"It's not easy losing someone you love," Kurt said quietly. He touched her cheek, wiping away a stray tear with his finger.

"No. No, it's not." Andrea exhaled on a shaky sigh. "And her death was..."

Kurt waited patiently for her to finish, his arms tightening around her, offering reassurance.

"Such a waste." Andrea crumpled the bandanna into a tight wad. "You know, it's funny. I was forever giving Dee a hard time because she always lived for the moment. I'd insist she make plans for her future, but she'd just laugh and say, 'Later, Andrea, later.' I wonder if somehow, deep down, she knew."

Kurt shook his head. "No, she didn't. She couldn't have. And you shouldn't ask yourself these questions. They'll just make you miserable. I'm sure Dee wouldn't have wanted that."

Andrea lifted her head. "What about you—what you're still going through? Would Sarah want to see you suffering? That's just as pointless as her death—or Dee's."

"What do you want me to do? Let Sarah's death remain a mystery?"

"Let Sarah rest in peace."

"I have to know, Andrea. *I* can't rest until I do."

Andrea took in a deep breath. "I'd like to help."

Kurt's chin jerked up at that. "How?"

"I could keep my eyes and ears open for you. I know I'm new around here, but that could work in my favor. People might talk to me about Sarah because I didn't know her, because I could be objective. I might hear something that'll help. If you'll let me."

An unreadable expression appeared in Kurt's eyes. "After Dee's death, getting involved with Sarah's should be the last thing you'd want. Why are you willing to do this?"

"Because I understand," she said simply.

Kurt said nothing for a moment. "I should get back to my tent."

"Don't forget your mail."

"Right." But he made no move to retrieve his envelopes, or to shift Andrea from his lap. "You know, you never did tell me if there was anyone special in your life right now."

"We did get sidetracked, didn't we?" Andrea said with a wistful smile.

"Well?"

Andrea looked into the face of her partner and suddenly found herself wanting to speak the truth.

"There's one man who has definite possibilities," she admitted.

"Oh." Kurt actually seemed disappointed. "I shouldn't be surprised," he finally said. "Of course there'd be someone."

His nearness stirred something deep inside. Andrea was weary of hiding her feelings, weary of being cautious. Life was too precious to waste in waiting for the right time, the right circumstances. The bandanna fell from her fingers as her hands reached up to clasp his neck. Her lips approached his.

"Can't you guess?" she whispered. "It's you."

As she kissed him, Andrea held nothing back. She savored the wondrous excitement that promised a beginning if she—if they—dared explore it. She was ready to embrace life again. More than ready.

But apparently Kurt wasn't. After only a moment's hesitation, he broke off the embrace, pushing her firmly away until they were no longer touching.

Andrea stared up at him, the hurt evident in her face. "Kurt?"

"This isn't right," he said harshly. He reached for his mail and stuffed it in his pocket, then grabbed his rain slicker.

"Why?" Andrea asked boldly. "You asked me if I was seeing anyone special. You had your arms around me! If that isn't a sign of interest, I don't know what is!"

Kurt jammed an arm through one sleeve and then the other. "You were crying and needed comfort. That's all it was."

"At first." Andrea noticed that he didn't meet her eyes.

"I'm an instructor, for heaven's sake! I wasn't trying to make a pass!"

"That's what you said the other night when you kissed me," Andrea retorted. "I didn't believe you then, and I don't believe you now. Kurt, we've done nothing wrong! You act as though a little tenderness is a hanging offense!"

Kurt's lips tightened. "You're forgetting our professional relationship. Throwing yourself at me is hardly acceptable behavior for a ranger-in-training."

Andrea gasped in shocked indignation, but then her eyes narrowed with understanding. "This isn't about our work. It's about you. You're afraid to take a chance on me because of Sarah."

"You don't know what you're talking about," Kurt said angrily.

"Yes, I do! We've both lost someone we loved. When Dee died, I decided to live every moment to its fullest. But when Sarah died—"

"You leave Sarah out of this!"

Andrea refused. "When Sarah died, you decided to play it safe. *That's* why you keep pushing me away! Kurt, I think we'd be good for each other, but we'll never know if you don't give me—give us—a chance!"

Kurt's expression was terrible to see. "I don't want anyone in my life again. Especially not you."

He unzipped the tent flap, and was gone.

CHAPTER EIGHT

"THE CURRENT IS speeding up," Andrea remarked, despite her earlier resolution to avoid unnecessary conversation with Kurt. "It's actually pulling on my oars."

It was early the next morning, and they were back on the Colorado River. The sun already burned brightly, but it hadn't chased away Andrea's depression over Kurt's rejection the night before. Their interaction so far had been strictly formal—senior instructor and trainee.

"That's why we have the oarlocks and carry spare oars. Most of the Grand Canyon's largest rapids are upriver. We'll be hitting them soon."

"When will we get to the white water?" Andrea asked, starting to feel a little excitement despite her gloom.

"At 52—Kwagunt."

"Pardon?"

Kurt looked over his shoulder but continued paddling. "All the rapids are marked by using the length of the Colorado as a reference. Lees Ferry, where we started, is officially Mile Zero. Pierce Ferry, at the end of the Canyon, is Mile 279.5. Kwagunt Rapids are found at Mile 52. Then come the Unkar and Hance Rapids at Mile 71 and 77, and so on. Not only does it help with navigation, but it helps with rescues."

"I see." Andrea filed away that bit of information. "Where are the biggest rapids?"

"Hermit Rapid and Crystal Rapid are two of the most famous. They're between Mile 95 and Mile 98, along with Tuna Creek Rapid and the Jaws of Death."

Andrea swallowed hard. "Jaws of Death?"

"Yes, but don't let the name fool you. Hermit Rapid is much scarier. So is Crystal. In fact, Crystal Rapid is so popular that practically everyone hikes the land trail to the head of Crystal Creek to run it." A pause. "Sarah loved Crystal. It was her favorite."

Andrea said nothing. She was beginning to hate the name of Sarah Wolf. She was also beginning to suspect that when Sarah died, not just one but two lives had been lost.

Kurt still paddled steadily. "It's quite a ride. We can run it if you want."

"I don't know..." Andrea's voice trailed off as she watched the rhythm of Kurt's oars.

"That isn't where she went under, in case you're worried about it," Kurt said calmly, his back still toward her. "So if you want to do Crystal, I really don't mind."

"I'm not Sarah," Andrea replied stiffly. "And I'm no thrill seeker. To be honest, I'm more interested in the Indian ruins than in the rapids. I read there's over five hundred pueblo and cliff dwellings inside the Canyon and over twenty-five hundred archeological sites. I'd rather be on my feet exploring than sitting all day in a raft."

"So would I," Kurt said, facing her again. "I haven't seen all the ruins I've wanted to, either. But you haven't experienced your first big rapid yet. You may change your mind."

"Not me. I hate surprises. Calm and controlled is my motto."

Kurt obviously wasn't convinced. "We'll see. We'll be hitting our first white-water patch in a little while."

Andrea was apprehensive but felt as prepared as possible. Kurt had lectured her carefully on how to run rapids.

"Just follow my lead," he was saying now. "If I steer toward a white patch of water, that means we're going nose over it. If I steer away from it, I want you to let the raft pivot around the dead water. Let your end swing around and away. It's easier than a diagonal retreat. If you're in doubt, don't paddle at all. Got it?"

"Got it."

"Make sure your life jacket is fastened securely and your knees are wedged in tightly under your safety strap. If for some reason you get thrown—"

"Like if the raft flips?"

Kurt looked as if he expected to see a total eclipse sooner. "Or you fall out. If you find yourself in the water, don't fight your progress downstream. That's the biggest mistake you can make. If you try to grab at a rock or push yourself away from one, you'll end up breaking an arm. We've got helmets that'll protect our heads, so go with the current. Eventually you'll clear the rapids and end up in calmer water."

"So I should just swim to shore and wait for you?"

"Right. The main thing is to not panic. The rides on even the longest rapids aren't more than three to four minutes long. If you keep a clear head and concentrate on getting your air without choking, you'll be okay."

"I think I'd rather concentrate on staying in the raft," Andrea said decisively.

"Smart lady. Now repeat everything I've said back to me."

Andrea did, to Kurt and then mentally to herself as they approached the white water. She was certain she was ready—but nothing could have prepared her for the sheer power, speed and exhilaration of the Colorado.

The force of the water struck her in the face with a strength that both frightened her and gained her respect. Her ears were filled with the roaring of the rapids, magnified from their earlier distant hissing. Kneeling, she tucked her thighs even tighter under the safety strap and focused on steering.

Many times she became disoriented from the spinning of the raft or the water in her face. She then did as Kurt ordered, letting him take control. His strength battled with the power of the Colorado; his bare shoulders and arms strained with the effort of enforcing his will on the river. And as Andrea saw that Kurt was more than a match for it, she realized one thing. For the first time in her life, she'd found someone she trusted implicitly.

That realization shook her as much as her first whitewater rafting experience did. By the time Kurt had steered them into calmer waters and was paddling toward shore, Andrea was breathless.

"Well?" he asked. "What did you think?"

She shook her head. "Wow."

Kurt smiled for the first time that day, the warmth reaching his eyes. "Kind of takes your breath away, doesn't it?"

Andrea nodded, and pushed some straggling hair out of her face.

"Still voting to explore those Indian ruins?"

"I think I need something less strenuous right now, like collapsing on the sand." Andrea drew in a shaky breath. Her shoulder muscles were twitching with fatigue; her back ached from the effort of maintaining her balance.

Kurt's paddle struck bottom, and he stepped into the shallow water and pulled the raft onto the beach.

"Here we are." He checked the diver's watch he wore. "It's after two. We can have lunch and then set up camp for the day."

"Sounds good to me." Andrea released the oar, her fingers numb from clenching, and threw one leg over the edge of the raft. Her thigh muscle cramped, her leg buckled, and she spilled face first into the water.

Immediately Kurt's hands were around her waist, lifting her first to her feet, and then up into his arms. His eyes were on her as she grabbed at her thigh.

"Hurts bad?" he asked with sympathy.

"Like the devil. I told you I'm not used to sitting. Or kneeling." She grimaced.

He set her down gently on the beach and began to rub her thigh. "Most trainees fall out of their rafts in the rapids. You're the first one I've had who waited to do it in two feet of water," he said lightly.

"Very funny. Ow, that hurts!" Andrea slapped at the cramp with her palm as it knotted even tighter.

"Well, if you'd move your hands, I could get rid of it," Kurt said.

"No, thanks." She pushed his fingers off her bare leg and continued her massaging. "I'll get rid of my own cramp."

Kurt frowned. "Come on, Andrea, let me help. This is no time to go shy on me."

"I'm not being shy." Andrea gritted her teeth. "I just don't want to be accused of throwing myself at you again."

"Give me some credit," he said tersely. "Even you can't develop leg cramps on demand." He reached for her thigh again.

Andrea immediately pushed him away with her good foot. "Go away!"

"Gladly, once I take care of this. Now move your hands out of the way or so help me..."

He didn't finish the threat, but the tone of his voice made Andrea obey. She averted her head as he massaged her thigh.

"Just stay still and hold on. Another few seconds and— there!" he said with satisfaction. "I can't feel a knot anymore."

Andrea blinked. The sharp pain had stopped. "It's gone," she said in surprise.

Kurt removed his hands from her leg, and Andrea breathed a sigh of relief. Now that she was feeling better, she noticed how disturbingly close he was.

"Thanks for—" She abruptly broke off, her eyes opening wide as he lifted his hands to her cheeks and cupped her face.

Kurt's mouth approached hers. "You're welcome," he murmured, placing a gentle kiss on her lips. And then, before Andrea had time to respond, he drew back. She stared at him with frank amazement, unsure of what to say or how to react. The only thing she knew for certain was that she wanted more. . . .

Kurt released her face, then tapped the bottom of her chin. "Close your mouth," he said with a smile.

Andrea deliberately turned away to hide her confusion, and prayed Kurt would stand up and start unloading the raft. Her prayers went unanswered. He settled himself more comfortably beside her.

"You look a fright," he said conversationally. "Where's that compact now?"

Andrea's hand went immediately to her hair. She knew it wasn't as smooth or shining as usual. There was little clear water in the Canyon, for the Colorado continued to cut deep into the earth, just as it had in prehistoric times. Andrea's formerly white canvas sneakers were now the same silty red as the river, while her hands and legs were smeared with the bank's muddy soil.

She opened her mouth for a tart response, then saw the twinkle in his eyes. He was teasing her! She tried to whip up her anger again and keep it alive, but she couldn't. It just melted down until it was gone.

"My compact's packed away," she said lightly. "I'll have to make a few minor repairs later."

"Don't. I like you better like this."

Andrea turned toward him with disbelief. "Tired, wet and covered with mud?"

"Yes."

Andrea forced back the grin she felt inside. "Well, there's no accounting for taste. But since you got me out of those monstrous rapids in one piece, I'll allow it."

Kurt laughed. "Those were just baby rapids. If you want, we can hike to Lava Falls at Mile 179—near the middle of the Canyon. It's the largest rapid here."

"Why's it called Lava Falls?"

"Because there's an old volcano cone right in the center of the white water."

"You want me to go out of my way to risk smashing myself into a volcano? Right smack in the middle of the Canyon's biggest rapid? Thanks for nothing. I'll pass."

"Scared?"

"Let's just say I have a very high regard for my unbroken bones."

Kurt accepted her answer, and didn't try to press her. "How's your leg?" he asked.

Andrea rubbed her thigh. "A little sore, but getting better. A couple more minutes here and it'll be fine."

"That'll give me time to recover from that kick you gave me."

"It was *not* a kick. It was just a shove." But Andrea couldn't hide the sparkle in her eyes. "You should have moved when I asked you."

"And people say *I* have a temper."

Andrea decided to ignore that remark. For now, she was grateful that the tension of earlier had disappeared. She remained silent, watching the occasional raft float by, the passengers still gasping and gaping at the trip they'd just made.

Kurt stretched his legs out in front of him and crossed his ankles. The water lapped at his bare feet. "You know, many of the popular rapids aren't on the Colorado itself,'' he explained. ''They're on the four major tributaries that empty into it. Which is one reason people have to get off the river and hike. The other is that much of the Colorado itself isn't navigable. You have to realize that from the start of the Canyon at Lake Powell to its end at Lake Meade, the riverbed descends almost two thousand feet.''

''No wonder the current's so dangerous.''

''Yes. With four tributaries, that's a lot of water speeding downriver. Everyone, including us, has to get off the river at different points. There are drops on the Colorado too deadly for even modern craft to survive.'' Kurt gestured toward the river before them. ''Think about what we just went through, then consider the earliest explorers of the Canyon. In 1869, it took John Wesley Powell three months to row down the Grand Canyon during his mapping expedition.''

''Three months? But we don't have motors, and it'll only take us a week.''

''Powell's expedition had to carry heavy wooden rowboats instead of inflatable rafts around the bad spots. And,'' Kurt went on, ''Powell only had one arm when he did it.''

''One arm? What happened to him?''

''He was a Civil War veteran, a major as a matter of fact. And a geologist and ethnologist. He wrote books on his travels.''

''I know.'' Andrea nodded. ''What he did took a lot of courage.''

''Those were harsh times, back then.''

''I suppose so,'' she said slowly. ''But somehow I feel they were simpler times.''

''Maybe. But in one way, life was no different. Then, like now, only the strong survived.''

She thought of Sarah, and of Kurt's refusal to let her go. "Physical strength isn't enough, Kurt. Strength also comes from the heart."

Kurt gave her a penetrating look, and said nothing.

The silence grew uncomfortably long. Sighing, Andrea rose to her feet. "It's getting late. Let's set up camp."

An hour later the two of them had put up the tents, changed into dry clothes, and were just finishing the last of their meal.

"So where will we end up tomorrow?" Andrea asked over her coffee. "How fast are we traveling?"

"We've made pretty good time," Kurt replied. "The big motorized rafts can cover forty miles a day and easily do the whole river in a week. We're somewhat smaller, but we're doing about twenty-five a day. We should make the Bright Angel Quadrangle tomorrow. There's a boat beach near the Kaibab Suspension Bridge right before Mile 88."

"I've been to that ranger station," Andrea remembered.

"Yes, it's one of our bigger ones. We'll stock up on fresh water and supplies and plan our next stretch of the trip."

"I still haven't see any ruins," Andrea said. "So far we've either been too tired to go, or it's rained."

Kurt looked up at the afternoon sky. "Looks like we're in for more bad weather, too. If this keeps up, we may have to cancel not only a visit to the ruins but our whole trip."

Obviously Kurt hoped so, Andrea thought. But her disappointment was mixed with hope. Maybe Kurt was suddenly uncomfortable around her because she'd made him reconsider his quest to clear Sarah's name. A little more time with him might even change his mind. She prayed for nice weather and the continuation of their rafting trip.

But the rain started coming down hard soon after and settled in for the next few days. Andrea was cold, silent and miserable on their voyage down the Colorado. She knew long before they reached the Bright Angel station that the rafting expedition was over. The only silver lining in this was the fact that she wouldn't have to raft down the stretch of river that had claimed Sarah Wolf.

"We'll have to postpone," Kurt said as they stowed their raft and gear in the ranger station's storage shed. It was late afternoon and still raining. "I can't in all conscience go out again. We'll finish up that part of your training when the weather clears."

Andrea hoped that was true. On rafting trips, there were no real off-duty hours. Would Kurt risk her prolonged company again after all that had happened between them?

When the raft was deflated and packed away, and the packages of dried food back on the supply shelves, they trudged though the rain to the cabins at Phantom Ranch.

"Tomorrow we'll hike back up to the rim. Or if we're lucky, we can catch a mule ride back to the top," Kurt said as Andrea pulled her slicker drawstrings tighter. "With all this rain, they should have some cancellations."

Andrea nodded to show she had heard him, then shivered. She wasn't worried about a mule right now. She was more concerned with getting a hot meal, a hotter shower, dry clothes and a warm bed. And a phone, she suddenly remembered. Her mood lifted just a little. Emily and her family should be at the hotel at the top of the rim by now. She'd have to give them a call.

"It's getting late," Kurt said as Phantom Ranch's buildings came into view. "If we change now, we'll miss eating. We should hit the chow line first."

"That's fine with me." she was looking forward to a cup of hot, strong coffee.

They trudged up the stairs, rain slickers and backpacks dripping. Andrea threw back her hood as she stepped into the dimly lit chow hall. There were plenty of empty tables because of the storm.

Kurt paused to read the marquee menu above the serving counters. Andrea stopped at a table near the beginning of the chow line to take off her backpack and coat. She'd barely pulled her arms out of the sleeves when she heard her name yelled out in a delighted shriek.

"Emily?" Andrea was barely able to turn around before Emily hurtled into her arms with all the exuberance of the very young.

Andrea lifted the child up to give her a big hug. "Hi, sweetheart! What in the world are you doing here?"

Emily had her arms around Andrea's neck in a choke-hold that was a child's version of a hug. "We rode the mules down! Only it was raining and I didn't want to go. Now I'm glad I did!"

"Emily, get back over here," a woman scolded urgently.

Emily wasn't about to obey. "It's her, Grandma, it's her!" She wriggled out of Andrea's grasp, too excited to stay quietly in her arms. "Andrea's here!"

Andrea was touched by Emily's delight at seeing her again. As the girl hopped from one foot to the other, Andrea reached for her hand, saying, "Be careful, Emily. Remember your leg."

"It's fine. It hardly ever hurts." Emily stopped, raising her right leg in the air for Andrea's inspection. "See? No more cast!"

By now Emily's parents and grandparents had gathered around her. The chow hall was filled with exurberant words of welcome. Andrea wasn't able to get a word in edgewise, let alone silence the clamor. She just stood quietly with Emily's hand in hers, waiting for the noise to subside. It finally did at Kurt's approach.

"Andrea, I don't mean to interrupt," he said, "but they're about ready to close the chow line. Would you like me to get you something while you visit?"

"Please," Andrea said gratefully. The happy throng surrounding her wasn't about to let her go. "I'll have whatever you're having, and a cup of coffee to go with it."

Emily tugged at Andrea's hand. "Is this your partner? The one you told me about in your letter?"

Kurt answered the question directed toward Andrea. "Yes, I'm Kurt Marlowe, Andrea's instructor."

"Hi," Emily said shyly, staring up at Kurt's tall frame. "I'm Emily Jenkins."

"These are Emily's parents and grandparents," Andrea explained. Introductions were quickly made, the men shook hands, then everyone's attention was back on Andrea.

"Are you Andrea's neighbors from Denver?" Kurt asked politely.

"Andrea carried me out when I broke my leg," Emily piped up before anyone else could reply. "We met on the airplane. It crashed, you know."

Kurt looked sharply from the girl to Andrea.

"He doesn't know about that, Emily," Andrea said uneasily.

"You didn't tell him about the crash, and how you rescued my daughter?" Emily's father asked, his voice incredulous.

All eyes were on Andrea, including Kurt's. "You were in a plane crash?"

"Yes, this past winter, in Denver." Emily's grandfather reached into his wallet and withdrew a worn newspaper clipping. He unfolded it and held it out for Kurt to see. It showed Andrea barefoot in the snow, holding an injured Emily in her arms.

Behind her was the burning body of the plane. Andrea closed her eyes against the memory.

"If you'll excuse me, I need to get to my cabin." Andrea forced herself to take slow breaths.

"But I want to see you!" Emily insisted.

"After I change, okay, sweetheart?" Andrea could barely get the words out, and felt a rare anxiety attack coming on.

"Don't you want your dinner?"

"Later!"

Andrea ignored Emily's protests and Kurt's concerned look as she hurried to her cabin. If she could get away from those newspaper clippings she'd be okay. She just needed a few minutes alone.

But even as she entered her cabin, she knew it was too late. The events were already playing themselves over in her mind....

SIRENS WAILED as ambulances and fire engines raced to the passenger jet, its body broken and bleeding onto the icy runway.

"You're not going to die!" Andrea yelled to be heard above the screams.

"We are!" one man shouted back. "Just like that stewardess beside you!"

Andrea unfastened her belt and left her seat in the front of the plane's passenger section. She pulled her skirt away from the clutching fingers of another hysterical man, and forced herself to stop thinking about Dee. If she allowed herself to think about that, she'd start screaming too. She took in a deep, trembling breath.

"Calm down and listen, sir. The emergency chute is ready and waiting. Stand up, get your wife and walk to the rear of the plane." She pulled the passenger to his feet, placed his wife's hand in his and gave them both a push. "Go!"

Already she was turning to the next row and unbuckling the seatbelts of two other stunned passengers.

"Go to the rear of the plane and the emergency chute. I've got a couple of men there who'll help you down. Don't run, don't push, but keep moving," Andrea urged the aisle passenger, an elderly woman with a cane.

Andrea then yanked out her shirttail and swiped blood away from the eyes of the woman's seatmate, a heavily overweight businessman. "Come on, sir, you'll have to walk on your own. There's no one who can carry you."

The man looked up at her with his undamaged eye, then gazed forward. "The cockpit's gone. I—I can see the sk–sky!" He stuttered with confusion. "What happened? Where's the cockpit?"

"We crashed, sir. I don't know where the cockpit is. Now get up." Andrea tugged him to his feet, then slung his arm around an already standing male passenger. "Take this man to the chute. I don't care if you have to drag him by the hair, but keep this line moving!"

She was really shouting now, for the sirens were getting closer and the passengers sliding down the chute were screaming with pain and fear.

"I see fire!" a woman cried, and suddenly there was pushing and shoving to get to the exit.

"Slow down! Slow down!" Andrea yelled in her best drill-sergeant voice. She grabbed at a panicking teen and yanked him to a slower speed. "Take it easy. We still have time."

Andrea looked behind to where the cockpit once was, and where the flight attendants' seats framed the gaping hole... Where Dee had laughed and smiled... Where the flames were outlined against open sky...

Wake up, Dee! her mind screamed. *Wake up!* But Dee remained motionless in the seat next to Andrea's, and Andrea turned away, moving to the crying girl in the adjacent row.

"Come on, sweetie, stand up," Andrea ordered. "We have to go."

"My leg hurts," Emily whimpered.

Andrea looked down and saw the sharp edge of bone sticking out of flesh. She bit her lip.

"I'll carry you," she announced, seeing that everyone else was out of their seats and heading for the exit.

The flames roared up with a vengeance in the front half of the cabin, and Emily's eyes opened wide with fear. Andrea's throat tightened as she unclicked the seat belt. If there was time, she would have splinted the fracture. But time was a luxury they didn't have.

Andrea reached for the child. "This might hurt. But we've got to get out of here."

The moment she lifted her, Emily screamed and fainted in Andrea's arms. Andrea's mascara melted and dripped onto the child's face as hot black smoke filled the air. She kicked off her heels and hurried down the empty aisle for the rear emergency chute.

The flames reached the puddled jet fuel as Andrea jumped onto the neon yellow plastic of the chute. It sizzled into a bright fireball as her feet slammed onto concrete. Then she was running, running, running—Emily's dead weight hugged tight against her chest.

Andrea just reached the grassy edge of the runway when the explosion hit; its shock wave knocking woman and child to the snowy ground. Her ears filled with a pounding roar that blessedly stopped and was replaced with the fire engines' siren wails.

Emily opened her eyes, whimpered again, then started shaking.

Or were they both shaking?

Andrea couldn't tell. She struggled to a standing position, carefully cradling the child in her arms. She took Emily's hand into her own as she frantically looked around for something to use as a splint. It was minutes—an eternity—before she heard voices.

"Are you all right?"

I—I'm alive! I made it! Then the awful, other fact finally sank in. *Dee didn't....*

Paramedics approached them, while cameras were pointed at Andrea. One paramedic wrapped a blanket around her torn, soiled uniform and brushed the February snow off her arms.

"I heard you saved all the passengers!" Another reporter shoved a microphone in her face, while a burly security man tried to push it away.

Andrea ignored them all. The paramedics were gently pulling her hand away from Emily's, and the little girl cried out as she was loaded onto a stretcher. Andrea's nails bit into her palms at the sound.

"Miss—miss! Any comment?"

Andrea stared at the burning body of the plane on the runway. Hot, scorching tears spilled onto her cheeks.

"Please, miss, won't you say something for the cameras?"

Andrea shook her head and closed her eyes. *I just quit the business.*

CHAPTER NINE

LATER THAT NIGHT, Andrea was startled by a knock on her cabin door. She was ready to prepare for bed and had just untied one boot.

"Andrea, it's Kurt. May I come in?"

She stood up from her sitting position on the bed, her boot lace trailing. Much to her relief, Emily's family had finally left her cabin for their own. They'd shown up an hour or so after Andrea had run from the chow hall, their newspaper clippings discreetly tucked away. Andrea was glad to see Emily again, but the constant praise of the rest of the family had become uncomfortable.

She hadn't expected to see Kurt tonight. He'd come over with Emily's family and brought her a dinner of cold sandwiches and fruit, but he'd left soon after to take care of business at the ranger station.

"Come on in."

"It's late. Are you, uh, decent?" he asked from the other side of the threshold.

"Yes. I haven't had time to get ready for bed. Everyone just left. Please, have a seat."

Only then did Kurt enter and remove his rain slicker. He waited for Andrea to sit down on the bed before taking the tiny cabin's only chair.

"Are you okay?" he asked quietly.

"Of course I am. Why wouldn't I be?"

Kurt frowned, obviously not satisfied. "Andrea, you practically bolted out of the chow hall when they appeared.

It must have been rough, having Emily spring her whole family on you like that.''

"Perhaps a little.'' Andrea tucked her legs under her. "I met her parents at the hospital in Denver, but this was the first time I'd met the grandparents. Their enthusiasm over my rescuing Emily—'' Andrea shook her head in disbelief. "I never thought they'd still be carrying newspaper clippings around.''

"I imagine it was quite a shock to see those photos again.''

"It was,'' Andrea said ruefully. "But I'm okay now.''

"Why didn't you tell me?''

"Do you go around telling everyone about Sarah?''

Kurt's chin lifted. "Your friend Dee was on that flight?'' he asked with sudden comprehension.

"Yes.'' The admission came out on a sigh. "Dee was the other flight attendant—the flight's only fatality. Ironic, isn't it? A whole planeload of strangers, and the only person who dies is my best friend.''

Kurt got up to sit beside her on the bed, his face compassionate. "You should take your own advice and not dwell on things like that.''

"I usually don't, but seeing those clippings again...'' Her voice trailed off.

"Are you sorry they came?''

"No. I'm very glad I saw Emily. I wasn't able to help Dee, but I did help her. And the others.'' Andrea smiled. "That makes it a little easier.''

Kurt was silent for a moment. Andrea waited for him to speak of his own accord.

"I wish Sarah could have saved those three rafters,'' he finally said. "Maybe then her death wouldn't seem like such a waste.''

"Kurt, you can't mourn the dead forever.''

"Do you expect me and my daughter to go on just as though everything was normal?" he asked angrily.

"No," she said in a steady voice. "But you should be dwelling on life instead of death. And if you can't, then you're in the wrong job. Why can't you leave Sarah's death alone?"

Kurt looked her straight in the eye. "I'm hoping the truth will help Lynn, especially when she's old enough to understand."

"And you, Kurt? Will it help you?"

Kurt wouldn't—or couldn't—answer that question. He rose from the bed and headed for the door.

Andrea watched him with sad eyes. "Life is precious, Kurt, no matter what tragedies come our way. You can't live in the past forever."

"I'm not," he snapped. "Good night."

There was a heaviness in her heart as he walked out of her cabin. She cared so very much about him and she was sure he cared about her. He was unfailingly considerate—he tried to ease her grief, looked out for her on plane flights, even concerned himself with lost uniform hats and missed meals. But the ghost of Sarah always hovered in the background. To make matters worse, she suspected it was too late to turn back now—even if she wanted to.

The rain settled in for the next two days. Kurt and Andrea were assigned Bright Angel campground duty until the weather cleared and their rafting trip could be resumed.

The noise of the heavily falling rain prevented much conversation while they were working outside. Andrea was relieved; Kurt seemed uncomfortable talking to her, and she was miserable during his silences. At least the rain gave her time to think.

By the time it stopped, Andrea realized one thing. Kurt Marlowe's welfare meant more and more to her. Her feelings for him were like nothing she'd ever experienced. But

Sarah Wolf, and Kurt himself, were preventing her from acknowledging those feelings. For now, she had to be content to wait.

On the morning Andrea was to continue her rafting expedition, her emotions were still in turmoil.

"Ready to shove off?" Kurt asked.

"Whenever you are."

They pushed the raft into the water, Andrea entering first. Their oars pulled in tandem to maneuver into the mainstream of the Colorado's fast current.

"Let's hope we don't get any rain today," Kurt said as the raft quickly picked up speed. "From the look of those clouds, it could go either way."

Andrea was silent, and Kurt turned to face her.

"You're supposed to say something like, 'I hope it doesn't rain, either.'"

"You haven't exactly been seeking out my conversation," Andrea said honestly. "In fact, you've avoided me as much as possible. I never thought a person like you could be so—" She abruptly broke off.

"So what?"

"So afraid." She continued paddling. "Afraid of me, afraid of life. If I hadn't seen it for myself, I never would have believed it."

Andrea saw Kurt's fingers clench even tighter around his oar. "If I were you, I'd pay more attention to the water and less to analyzing my character," he said harshly. "We have another big set of rapids coming up."

"I'll be ready."

"See that you are. We'll be there before you know it."

Kurt was right. The next patch of white water was a hissing maelstrom of fury. Andrea's heart pumped wildly as she and Kurt maneuvered through the treacherous rapids. By the time they reached calmer water, every nerve in Andrea's body was on overload.

"You okay?" Kurt asked.

Andrea nodded, busy trying to catch her breath.

"I'm going to beach the raft. I need a break, and you look like you could do with one, too. Follow my lead."

In a few moments Andrea was sinking into the softness of the silty red mud on the shore. She welcomed the stability of solid ground with a sigh of relief that didn't go unnoticed by Kurt.

"The river's rougher and faster than usual. They must have opened the dam's spill gates becase of all the rain." He made no move to sit next to her. Instead, he surveyed the Colorado with a troubled expression.

"Are we going to cancel again?"

"I think it's wise, at least until they close the gates up-river. I wouldn't feel safe unless I had one of the larger motorized rafts."

"What do we do in the meantime? Set up camp and wait?"

"Either that or hike out. I'll radio in and have someone check on the conditions up at Glen Canyon Dam first. Then we can decide."

Kurt unpacked the waterproof ammunition case that held the powerful radio. "I'll climb above the river a bit," Kurt said. "The reception's no good this far down. You wait here."

Andrea watched Kurt climb to higher ground before she dragged the raft farther on to the beach. She decided to unpack the coffeepot and small butane stove. She might as well fix something hot to drink while she waited.

She had just located the fresh water and matches when Kurt called out.

"Don't bother with that," he told her while still approaching. "We don't have time."

Andrea stopped in dismay at the tone of his voice. "Why not? What's wrong?"

"We've got a rescue."

She froze for a second, then immediately started repacking the coffeepot. "Who and where?"

"There's a lone kayaker a few miles ahead. Headquarters says he's smashed his boat and is hanging on to some rocks mid-river."

"Is he injured?"

"The person who reported the accident thinks so." Kurt put away the stove. "There's a steep drop-off below with jagged rocks. All but the experts get out and hike around it."

Andrea frowned at the whitecaps on the few smooth patches of water. "Can we use the helicopters?"

Kurt shook his head. "It's too windy to get them up."

"What about our motorized river patrols?"

"They were on their way, but ran into problems. It appears Judy fell out of the boat."

"Oh, no!" Somehow Andrea wasn't surprised.

"Oh, yes. Dan's busy trying to rescue *her*. When it comes to the kayaker, we're it."

Andrea steeled herself for the task ahead. "How long is it going to take us to hike past the drop-off?"

"Not us, Andrea, you."

"You're splitting us up? Kurt, I've never even practiced a water rescue, especially not in the middle of white-water rapids!"

"I don't expect you to. But it'll take us a good forty-five minutes to hike downriver. Our victim might not last that long. I can reach him in ten by raft."

Andrea's heart skipped a beat. "By going over the drop-off yourself?"

"I can handle it. I'm no amateur. It'll be tricky, but I should be able to maneuver close enough to throw him a line."

"Are you out of your mind?" Andrea gasped. "That's a haphazard rescue at best. I should be onshore, and you should be anchored to a safety line!"

"We can do that as a backup measure if I miss him the first time. You'll hike down and meet me below the drop-off. If I don't have our kayaker, I'll be waiting for you onshore for our second attempt."

"If you both haven't drowned! Kurt, it's too risky!"

"It's a chance I have to take."

Kurt took a step toward the beached raft, but Andrea blocked his way.

"Oh, no. You have to protect more than the victim's life, Kurt. You have to protect your own!"

"I don't want this man to end up like Sarah! Every second counts."

"You're no good to him dead! This is against everything I've been taught, Kurt—everything *you* taught."

"I've also taught you this job has its risks. Now move aside."

Andrea firmly planted her feet in the silt. "Is that how Sarah died, taking unnecessary risks?"

Kurt's eyes blazed indignantly, but Andrea refused to give ground.

"This river is full of drop-offs," she continued. "You told me Sarah drowned near one. Did she think it was best to take the quickest route, no matter what the danger?"

Kurt's face blanched. "Of course not," he managed to say. "She knew better than that. I *taught* her better than that."

"Then follow your own rules!"

"I make my own rules. I'm an expert in these waters!"

"And maybe Sarah thought she was too!"

There was a stricken silence on Kurt's part.

"I won't let you do this, Kurt. We'll both hike down to the other side of the drop-off. We stay together, and we rescue the kayaker together."

"No. My decision is final."

Andrea felt her heart grow cold. She knew he'd never listen to her, but this time Kurt was wrong! *She* was right.

She took a slow, deliberate breath. "All right, Kurt. Whatever you say."

Kurt walked a few yards away from her and gave the rapids a calculating glance.

"Just let me get my first-aid kid out."

Kurt nodded, and Andrea hurried over to the raft. But instead of grabbing the medical kit, she reached for the oars, slipped them out of the oar locks, and immediately hurled them far out into the river.

Kurt's head jerked around. "Damn you!" He lurched toward her, but Andrea already had the spare oars in hand. With a speed born of desperation, she eluded his grasp and sprinted ahead to the waterline.

"Andrea, don't!" Kurt yelled, but Andrea ignored him.

With a might heave, she pitched the spare oars into the water, watching as the current snatched them into its grasp and they disappeared.

Kurt grabbed her shoulder, whirling her around with a strength that hurt.

"You damn fool! Do you know what you've just done?"

Andrea triumphantly lifted her chin. "You bet I do."

His eyes blazed with fury and he shook her once, hard.

Andrea met his gaze with a fury of her own. "Let me go. We have a victim to rescue. You're wasting valuable time."

"You're the one who's wasted it!" Kurt snarled, but his hands dropped away from her, clenching into fists. "All right, Andrea. I have no choice but to do it your way. Get the winch and rescue harness, and let's go."

A few minutes later they were hurrying downstream. It wasn't an easy hike. Sometimes the beach disappeared into sheer canyon walls, and they had to hop carefully from boulder to slippery boulder above raging waters. Then came the descent, where the Colorado dropped steeply into a furious waterfall.

Andrea scrabbled for handholds as she and Kurt climbed down. The spray from the rushing waters hit her in the face, but it was easier to deal with that than the nervous feeling in her stomach. The cascading tons of water created by the narrow bottling and sheer drop of the canyon floor was frightening to behold. Just thinking of Kurt attempting to brave that waterfall made her physically ill. She had to look away.

Kurt reached the lower level of the bank first, but Andrea was right behind him.

"Did you see him?" Kurt had to yell into her ear to be heard above the noise of the water.

Andrea shook her head, ashamed that she hadn't been able to look for the kayaker while descending.

"He's over there!"

Kurt grabbed her arm and dragged her down the bank, then pointed. There, in the middle of the white water, was a splash of life-vest orange below a white helmet.

Andrea nodded her head in an exaggerated motion to show that she had heard. Then they dropped their packs. She started to set up the winch and rope with hands that were much steadier than her heart. Kurt pulled on the rescue harness over his life jacket, which he hadn't removed for the hike, and tightened his helmet.

The water continued to pound over the rocks, its volume deafening. Kurt hooked the harness up to the winch. "You remember how to operate this?" he yelled to her.

"Yes."

Kurt took the slack line in hand and approached the foaming edge of the water.

"Be careful!" Andrea yelled.

Kurt gave her a thumbs-up, then plunged into the torrent.

Andrea slowly plied out his line, careful not to twist or snag it. The current was hard and fast, but Kurt had angled his approach to have the best chance of reaching the kayaker. Even so, Andrea saw that Kurt was almost swept past the kayaker's rock. Only by repeated, powerful strokes was he able to get there.

Andrea held her breath as Kurt attached the kayaker to his line. She was still holding her breath when he waved. That was her signal to bring them back. She reeled them both in, the winch straining against the power of the river. Slowly but surely, the two men finally approached the shore.

As soon as Kurt's feet hit the bank, a relieved Andrea was by his side to help haul the man in. The victim's eyes fluttered, and he collapsed immediately upon reaching land.

"His leg's broken," Andrea said, immediately noticing the contorted angle.

"His right arm, too, I think," Kurt added as they carried the kayaker higher up on the shore.

Andrea was ready with the emergency aid kit. "Why don't I take care of him while you get back on the radio?" she suggested. Kurt might be the senior ranger, but her emergency medical technician's training was much more extensive than his first-aid background. She was glad he recognized the one area where she had more expertise; he stepped aside.

"If we can't fly this man out, we'll need a boat—not mules. He can't ride while he's unconscious," she said frankly. "And with two broken limbs I don't want the mules dragging him out."

"I'll see what I can do," Kurt promised. "Do you need any help with those splints?"

"No, but bring me some towels and a blanket after you radio in."

"Will do."

Andrea worked quickly and confidently. By the time Kurt hiked back down to her, she'd done all she could for her patient.

"Help should be here anytime," he said. "A commercial motorized raft is off-loading its passengers for the afternoon. They'll help us transport this man to the Bright Angel station."

"Do they have a stretcher?" Andrea asked. She knew they'd have to take the kayaker to a calmer area where a large raft could beach.

"Yes, and two other rangers who'll help us carry him."

"Judy and Dan?"

"No. There wasn't any news on them yet."

Andrea bit her lip and said a small prayer for her friend.

"How's our patient doing?" Kurt asked.

"He's still unconscious. But his pulse is strong, and his color's improved."

"Then I'll leave him in your hands. I'm going to deflate our raft. With the extra help, we'll be able to transport both the patient and our gear to the ranger station. We'll check for news on Judy there."

Andrea tucked the blanket more tightly around the kayaker. She wasn't sorry to see the trip come to an end. "The Colorado can be cruel, can't it?"

Kurt gave her a sharp look. He didn't comment, but those words came back to haunt her when the two other rangers arrived.

"Isn't that Earl?" Andrea asked as the relief help came into sight. "The one who gave us our mail?"

"Yes," was all Kurt would say, but Andrea saw the tension in his shoulders when Earl and his partner approached with the stretcher.

"The raft's about a five-minute hike downstream," Earl announced. "Is the patient strong enough to move?"

Andrea once more checked the kayaker's vital signs. "I think so. He's pretty stable, considering his injuries."

Earl placed the stretcher on the ground next to the kayaker, and the four of them carefully moved the unconscious man onto it. "Do you know how this happened?"

It was Kurt who answered. "He went over a drop-off he should have hiked around. Just like Sarah did. Right, Earl?"

Earl didn't answer. Andrea's fingers froze, suspended above their task of securing the stretcher's straps.

"I never said that," Earl said in a voice that deceived no one.

"But it's the truth. That's how she must have died. It all makes sense—Jim's silence, yours, everyone's."

Earl's expression gave him away.

Kurt swallowed hard before saying, "I wonder why I didn't figure it out before."

"How *did* you find out?" Earl asked in a compassionate voice. "Did someone finally tell you after all this time?"

Kurt shook his head. "It was something Andrea said."

Andrea looked at both men with disbelief, her chest tightening at the sight of Kurt's pain. She'd suspected for some time that Sarah had accidentally caused her own death, but it was still a shock to hear her suspicions confirmed.

"I'm sorry, Kurt," Earl said quietly. "We all are."

There was silence while everyone waited for Andrea to finish strapping in the kayaker. She ducked her head and hurried to complete the task.

"Why didn't you tell me, Earl?"

"Sarah's partner tried to talk sense into her during that rescue. He wanted to hike around the drop-off, but Sarah would have none of it. She said it was a waste of time. When her partner couldn't convince her otherwise, she went ahead without him."

"And then?"

Earl reluctantly continued. "The river drops more than forty feet there into a pile of rocks and a wicked undertow. Maybe someone like you could make it over, Kurt. But Sarah never had a chance. Those boaters didn't, either."

"So you all agreed to hide the truth?" He seemed to force the words from his lips. Andrea desperately wished she could be holding Kurt's hand instead of her patient's wrist.

"We all agreed to spare Sarah's family," Earl insisted. "Jim thought it would be easier for her parents—and for you and Lynn especially—to believe she died a hero's death instead of..."

"Instead of what?"

Earl hesitated, then said, "A wasted one."

Kurt swayed visibly. Earl started to reach for his shoulder, but Kurt savagely brushed him off. He grabbed one end of the stretcher, and after a moment, Earl did the same. Andrea and the other man lifted the rest of the gear. They all began the laborious hike over the rocks to the waiting raft.

By the time they reached the beach ramp of the nearest landing station, the wind had died down enough for a helicopter evacuation. The kayaker and Kurt's river gear were loaded aboard. Earl used the helicopter's radio to find out that Dan and Judy were now safely ashore. Andrea was relieved to hear that the helicopter would also pick up Judy—uninjured but badly shaken. The raft went back to its paying customers, and Earl and his partner prepared to hike back up toward the rim. Andrea and Kurt were to stay on the Canyon floor and report to the nearest ranger station.

"If it helps, Kurt, everyone respects your skills as a trainer," Earl said before leaving. "The only one responsible for Sarah's death is Sarah herself. She should never have taken such a chance."

Kurt was silent. He sat down on a rock, watching as the other ranger team hiked away. And eventually, they were alone, with just the Colorado for company.

Andrea longed for the words to console him, but knew that nothing she could say would help. Instead, she placed a comforting hand on his arm. At her touch, he turned to face her. She could tell that he was fighting for control, but at least he didn't shake her off.

"It's ironic, isn't it? An upstart flight attendant learns in two months what I've spent two years trying to find out." His eyes were dark with emotion. "My God, Andrea, am I the *only* one who didn't know?"

Andrea sat down and put her arms around him. She hugged him tight, remembering how he'd held her when she'd cried over Dee. Remembering how much he'd helped her. And praying she could do the same for him.

"Kurt, I'm so very sorry." She leaned her cheek against his hair. "I *didn't* know, not really. But everything about Sarah finally made sense, and when you insisted on going over that drop-off, I just said the first thing that popped into my head. That's why I threw the oars away. I had no idea—" Andrea drew in a painful breath. "I never meant to hurt you."

"I don't blame you." Kurt lifted his chin and met her gaze. "I'm glad I finally know."

"Are you?"

"Yes. Lynn and I deserve the truth, no matter how painful it is. I don't want Lynn's life to be built on lies. It's not fair to us, or to Sarah. So don't feel bad, Andrea. You said you'd help me, and you have."

Andrea felt some of the tightness in her throat dissolve. She took both of his hands into her own. The two of them sat quietly on the rock, watching the river.

"What now, Kurt?" Andrea asked as he become more composed. "What will you do now?"

"Go home for a while, I suppose. Take care of my daughter. Talk to her about her mother—about the happy times the three of us shared. I haven't been able to talk to anyone, even Lynn, about Sarah." Kurt's eyes were sad.

"Lynn needs to hear that Sarah loved her very much," he went on. "And when she's older, Lynn needs to know that Sarah was a ranger who tried her best, but overestimated her abilities. I want to be the one who tells her that."

"It won't be easy," Andrea said, her heart swelling with admiration for his courage. It would have been easier for everyone to believe that Sarah had died a hero's death.

"No. But I feel it's the right thing to do. I don't want Lynn to grow up with some hyped-up super-ranger image of Sarah. I want her to know the real Sarah, the woman I fell in love with. I'm sure Sarah herself would rather Lynn knew the real person, flaws and all, than some fantasy mother."

Andrea nodded. "When are you leaving for home?" she asked, hating to see him go, yet knowing he must.

"Tomorrow, probably. I'll find someone else to finish your training." Kurt slowly withdrew his hands from hers, once more the instructor.

"I'd rather wait until you returned."

"No." And now Kurt did stand.

"But—"

He interrupted her. "We should get back to Bright Angel and see if we can catch a mule ride to the rim. I'll have to go see Jim at personnel."

"Why—oh." Andrea suddenly remembered Judy. She hated the abrupt change of subject. She wanted to talk to Kurt about the two of them, about their relationship, their future—but Judy *was* her friend. She tried to put in a few good words for her.

"You're going to talk to Jim about Judy, aren't you? I can't say I'm surprised, but she's tried so hard. Kurt, maybe if you were training her, instead of Dan, she'd have a chance. Do you think you—"

"Andrea, I'm not talking about Judy."

"You're not? But then..." Andrea experienced a sudden feeling of foreboding.

"Judy's not the one who's leaving," Kurt said grimly. "I am."

"For good?" Andrea gasped, her knees going weak. She was glad she was still sitting on the rock. "Must you?"

"I told you once before that I was considering a job in Phoenix. Now that I know the truth about Sarah, there's nothing to stop me."

Not to see Kurt? Not to see his face or hear his voice every day? Andrea fought against the sudden panic.

"Why Phoenix? Why not Flagstaff?" she asked, striving to keep the desperation out of her voice.

"Phoenix is where my parents live."

Kurt's answer made sense, but something in his tone made her eyes narrow skeptically. "That's true. But an environmental protection group for the Canyon would base their operations in Flagstaff, the nearest city. Flagstaff's only fifty miles away from the Canyon, while Phoenix is three times that distance."

"Phoenix is the state capital. You have to expect the protection agency to have an office there also."

"To solicit funds from the government, yes. But I'd bet my last cent that's not what you're going to be doing."

"No."

Andrea rose slowly from her perch. "You should be working in Flagstaff. You don't *have* to work in Phoenix," she said with conviction. "What did you do, Kurt? Make a special request for that office so you could get away from here?''

No answer.

"So you could get away from *me*?'' Andrea's voice broke on the last word.

"Andrea, just drop it,'' Kurt replied wearily. "Lynn's the reason I'm leaving. You have very little to do with my decision.''

"I don't believe you! You're afraid to stay here. You're afraid to feel again! To care again! And I make you feel, don't I, Kurt?''

Kurt's eyes glittered. "Anger and frustration, Andrea. Nothing more.''

"Liar.'' She reached for him and drew his head down to hers. Her lips touched him, even as he'd touched her heart. Deep down, she knew he wouldn't resist.

He didn't. His words might deny the truth, but his welcoming arms couldn't, not when they were together. His response was just as honest, just as impassioned as hers. Their kiss whispered of a future that could be theirs. They were more than just physically attracted to each other. They were soul mates in the truest sense of the word—or could be, if Kurt allowed the icy numbness in his heart to melt.

Sarah's death had caused it. Andrea knew she could restore him to life with her love's warmth, if only Kurt would let her.

She felt the sudden change in him as he broke away.

"I can't, Andrea.''

"Why? Because of me?''

"Because of Sarah. Because it's my fault she's dead. If I'd trained her better, made her understand—'' His voice broke. "Maybe she'd still be alive today. Maybe I'm not cut out to be an instructor anymore.''

"Do you really believe that?'' Andrea asked incredulously. "Or do you just want *me* to believe it?''

She stared at him in silence, her eyes sorrowful and accusing. She hated what she was thinking, but couldn't help herself. Kurt was using any excuse, *anything*, to put distance between them.

Under her gaze, Kurt began to speak again. Then he shook his head and started toward the trail.

After a moment, Andrea followed with a heavy heart. Kurt was throwing away something valuable.

And they both knew it....

CHAPTER TEN

"JIM, YOU CAN'T ACCEPT Kurt's resignation! He's got some crazy idea that he could have prevented Sarah's death. We have to stop him!"

Andrea was in Jim Stevens's office. She'd gone there immediately after Kurt's own visit with the personnel director.

"I'm recommending you for a permanent position, Andrea," Kurt had said. "I know your sixty days isn't over yet, but I've seen enough to know you'll make a good ranger. I'll have Jim arrange your helicopter training right after I leave."

Andrea's clenched her fists just thinking about Kurt's words.

"We have to make him see reason, Jim," she insisted. "He says he was a bad example for Sarah. He thinks that's why she died."

Jim motioned her to a chair, but she was too upset to sit.

"You have to take chances as a ranger, Andrea. And the better you are at your job, the more risks you can safely take. Sarah was skilled, but she was no white-water expert like Kurt. She took risks on the Colorado she shouldn't have."

"Exactly," Andrea said with relief at Jim's understanding. "Only Kurt doesn't see it that way. We've got to do something to get him back!"

"I've tried talking to him, Andrea, but he's determined to quit. I did put him down for a leave of absence, but that's only effective for a short time." He shrugged. "After that, I have to abide by his wishes."

"How long can you stall his resignation?"

"A week, easily. Perhaps two, but no more."

Andrea sank into a chair. "I still have time left on my probation. Can't you make him stay here and finish my training? Maybe I can talk some sense into him."

Jim shook his head. "He's recommended you for a permanent position, and I've already filed the paperwork. You're due to start training with the evac helicopters in—"

Jim checked his schedule. A smile spread across his face, a smile Andrea instantly understood.

"What?"

"Training doesn't start for another eight days. How would like those days off, Andrea?"

"But I don't have any vacation time coming."

"You wouldn't be on vacation. You'd still be on the clock." Jim steepled his hands in a satisfied gesture and leaned against the back of his chair. "I want you to stay with Kurt. Consider this a special assignment, if you will."

"You'll let me go after him?" Andrea asked with rising hope.

"Yes. He's leaving this afternoon for his parents' home. You have a week to talk him into coming back to us before you'll have to report for duty. We need men like Kurt. I can't afford to let him go."

Neither can I, Andrea thought.

She hurried to her room, intending to quickly change and pack. Those plans were interrupted by a knock on her door. Andrea opened it, surprised to see Judy standing there.

"I won't stay long," Judy said, seeing Andrea's clean clothes laid out on the bed. "I just wanted to say goodbye."

"You're leaving?"

Judy lowered her eyes. "I'm giving Jim my resignation. I'm no ranger. I want to leave before anyone gets hurt on my account."

Andrea nodded, and said gently, "Judy, it took a lot of courage to make that decision."

Judy looked up at that. "You helped, you know."

"Me?"

"Yes. You stood up for me when I first started here. I've decided it's time to stand up for myself. I'm going home to Flagstaff, and I'm getting my old job back. I'm also going to report my boss for harassment."

"Good for you!"

Judy smiled. "I miss working at the bank. I hated leaving." She paused. "Despite everything, I don't regret coming here. I met you, and I met Dan. He and I, well, we—"

Andrea watched in amazement as Judy blushed and stammered. Judy and Dan, a happy match? Finally she managed to say, "If that's what you want, Judy, I'm very happy for you."

Some of Andrea's reticence much have showed.

"He's not so bad, once you get to know him," Judy said. "Dan's moving out of the ranger quarters. He and I are moving to Flagstaff to be near my old job."

"He doesn't mind?" Andrea asked in amazement. That sounded strange, the chauvinistic Dan making allowances for a woman.

"No." Judy shook her head vigorously. "Dan's glad he doesn't have to worry about me getting hurt as a ranger. He's quitting, too, so I won't have to worry about him, either."

Andrea blinked. "Does Dan at least have a job?" She hoped Judy wouldn't have to support them both.

"Oh, yes. He's going to work as a personal trainer at a Flagstaff health club. Isn't that great?"

"Yes, it's wonderful. Dan was always one for, um, staying in shape." Privately, she thought that a health club was the perfect place for Dan to flex his muscles.

Judy smiled at Andrea's remark. "He is, isn't he? He's all for the move, and me getting my old job back. The hours are so much better, and we'll have lots of time together."

Andrea wondered if all that time together would be such a good thing, but she felt a surge of envy at Judy's happiness just the same. Judy was so sweet tempered, she might even reform her black sheep.

"I wish you—and Dan—the very best, Judy. Thanks for stopping by."

Judy gave Andrea an impulsive hug. "You, too. You deserve it. Goodbye. Good luck!"

Good luck...

When it came to luck, Andrea wasn't much of a believer. Perseverance was more her style, and she'd need plenty of it to stop Kurt from leaving.

That spurred her to finish packing. Then, overnight bag in hand, she hurried to the rangers' private parking lot. She planned to remain by Kurt's Jeep to make certain she didn't miss him. She didn't have to wait long.

"Aren't you supposed to be at work?"

"I'm through for today." Andrea watched as he loaded two suitcases and a cardboard box into the back. "That isn't much gear for a man who's quitting."

"Not quitting. *Resigning*—to take care of my daughter," Kurt tersely corrected. "And I've always traveled light." He glanced down at her own suitcase, then back at her face. "So, it appears, do you. Are you going home for a visit?"

"Not me," Andrea replied. To Kurt's evident surprise, she placed her bag beside his things. "I'm going with you."

Kurt reached into the Jeep, removed her bag and dropped it at her feet. "I don't remember asking you along," he said bluntly.

"You didn't. Jim sent me. I don't start training with the helicopters for a week. I have that long to convince you to stay." Andrea defiantly replaced the suitcase inside the Jeep, then repeated Jim's earlier words. "Consider this a special assignment, if you will."

Kurt's mouth set in a hard line. "You have no business interfering in my personal life."

"Jim ordered me to go with you. He thinks you're making a big mistake." She opened the door and climbed in, then fastened her seat belt. "I happen to agree with him, by the way. And even if I didn't, you should know by now that I follow orders. I won't do anything to jeopardize my probation."

His eyebrows rushed together in anger. "I don't have time for your convoluted logic, Andrea. Get out of my Jeep."

"Uh-uh. You'll have to drag me out."

For a minute Kurt looked as though he was actually contemplating it, but Andrea didn't waver. Finally he closed her door and climbed into the driver's seat. They pulled out of the parking lot in silence.

The silence continued until they were clear of the park and heading down Route 180 toward Interstate 17, the main highway into Phoenix.

"I can't believe Jim actually sent you with me," Kurt said angrily. "You're wasting your time. I'm not going to change my mind."

"Maybe you won't, but I still have to try."

"Because of your *job?*"

"Because I think it's wrong for you to quit! Kurt, you weren't going to resign yet—and then you found out about Sarah. You were going to wait until your daughter started

school, remember? Sarah's death isn't reason enough to
leave behind untrained students."

"It is. Obviously, I'm a dangerous example."

"No, you're not! So you go over rapids few of the staff
ever attempt. You've been here ten years and you've got the
skill to do it."

He nodded. "It's something most people, including
Sarah, should never even try. I've emphasized that time and
time again. After all my warnings, I never thought she'd do
that, especially on her own."

"You're letting Sarah's death chase you away from a job
you love!" Andrea said firmly. "A job where you're
needed! You can't do that!"

"You're forgetting about my daughter," Kurt threw back.
"*She* needs me. And I need her."

"You need her for an excuse, you mean! An excuse to run
away!"

Andrea heard Kurt's indrawn breath of anger, but she
refused to stop. "You could easily move to Flagstaff. They
have schools in Flagstaff, and day-care centers, too. You
yourself told me your parents were getting too old to take
care of Lynn. There's no good reason for you to move so far
away."

"Has it ever occurred to you that this place has bad
memories for me?"

"They couldn't be *that* unbearable!" Andrea scoffed.
"You stayed at the Canyon for two whole years after
Sarah's death! You left your child behind in the process! So
don't expect me to believe a sudden paternal urge or a few
bad memories have you running like a scared rabbit. *You*
were the one who didn't want Lynn to grow up with lies.
Why don't you set her a good example? Be honest with
yourself!"

For a moment Andrea thought she'd gone too far. Kurt's
face grew taut with anger and his hands gripped the steer-

ing wheel tensely; for a moment she feared for their safety in the car. She was silent and anxious until Kurt calmed down and returned his attention to driving.

There was no more conversation for a while. They stopped halfway to Phoenix, in Sedona. Kurt bought gasoline and suggested a meal. Neither had eaten lunch, but neither had an appetite. They continued on to Phoenix without eating, and eventually reached the city limits.

"Are you still angry with me?" Andrea finally summoned up the courage to ask.

Kurt said nothing, and Andrea knew she had her answer.

"Next time I pull over I want you to call Jim," Kurt said tersely. "Tell him you rode with me into Phoenix, but couldn't change my mind. He won't be able to fault you for that. You can catch a bus back this evening. I'll drop you at the bus station before I go to my parents' house."

Andrea covered up her anguish at his eagerness to be rid of her. "I'm not going back," she decided. "Jim told me to stay in Phoenix, so I'm staying."

At least she had a better chance of seeing him again here in town. And Kurt hadn't rejected her personally. Until he confirmed her worst fear—that he wasn't leaving the Canyon because of Lynn or Sarah, but because of her—there was still hope. Andrea wasn't ready to give up yet.

"I'd rather you dropped me off at a hotel."

"A hotel?"

"Yes. I do have some time off. I might as well take advantage of it."

"What will you do?"

"I don't know. Maybe I'll go sight-seeing," she said with false bravado.

"Who with? Emily's grandparents? You don't have your car."

"I'll go by myself. I can buy a map and rent a car."

Kurt frowned. "I don't like you roaming around alone in a strange city."

"I'm an adult, and I'm quite capable of being on my own. I *am* disappointed, however. I was hoping to meet your family."

Kurt was silent, but Andrea boldly went on. He wasn't getting away from the Park Service—and her—without a fight.

"I'll be in town for the next week. Perhaps I can take you all out for dinner one night."

"You don't have to do that."

"I want to. I especially want to meet your daughter."

Despite the traffic, he turned toward her. "You want to see Lynn?" He sounded almost shocked.

"Is that so surprising? You've talked about her so much. I—I envy you."

Kurt faced the road again before he said, "I'm very lucky to have her."

"I'm sure she feels the same way about her father," Andrea responded quietly.

Kurt gave her one of his rare smiles. As she returned it, she felt a little of the tension between them disappear. His next words confirmed it.

"Perhaps you'd like to have dinner with us tonight? My parents love company."

"Even unexpected company?"

"Sure. They don't get out much."

"Then I'd be honored. Thank you, Kurt."

They were silent during the rest of the drive, but this time the silence wasn't uncomfortable. Andrea felt hope renew itself. It seemed that whenever she thought Kurt was about to cut any ties between them, he backed down. She prayed that maybe, just maybe, what she felt for him wasn't so one-sided.

Perhaps he could someday return the feelings she was now ready to acknowledge. She was in love with Kurt Marlowe. She wanted him to be part of her life, and she a part of his.

Kurt exited the interstate onto the slower, more sedate frontage roads. Andrea was surprised to see the citrus groves, their heavily irrigated lushness at odds with the wild desert cactus all around. Kurt said his parents lived on the northern outskirts of the city, where grapefruit and orange trees were cultivated.

"Dad decided he wanted to retire more or less in the country," Kurt explained.

"And your mother?"

"Mom still grows her cactus for customers. I don't think she'll ever completely give it up. She likes to keep busy."

Kurt stopped the car in front of a Spanish-style ranch house with a red tile roof. A small plant nursery was on the right, with the garage to the left.

Andrea saw an older woman with snowy white hair hurry out from the nursery.

"Your mother?" Andrea guessed.

"Yes." Kurt opened his door to his mother's waiting arms. He gave her a hug and a fond kiss on the cheek while Andrea climbed out of the car.

"I'm so glad you're here, Kurt. I wanted to call you, but—" Mrs. Marlowe noticed Andrea and suddenly broke off.

"Mother, this is Andrea Claybourne, a coworker of mine." Kurt quickly made the introductions. "Is something wrong?"

Mrs. Marlowe took in a deep breath. "Yes. Your grandfather Marlowe's very ill."

Kurt's lips drew together in a thin line before he asked, "How bad?"

"Bad enough. Your father's catching the next flight east. He wants me to go with him, and I'd like to see your granddad again. You know he's over ninety, and not very strong. But I don't have anyone to stay with Lynn.''

''So that's why you wanted to call me.''

Mrs. Marlowe nodded, her agitation plainly visible.

''I can stay with Lynn as long as you want, Mother.''

''Thank goodness,'' Mrs. Marlowe said with relief that quickly faded. ''But what about your job? And you have a guest. I don't know if you should.''

''I'm on a leave of absence, so there's nothing to worry about.'' Kurt's eyes warned Andrea not to say anything to the contrary. ''Hurry and pack, Mother. I'll tell Dad I'm here.''

Andrea was shown inside. Kurt disappeared to speak to his father, while his mother went to her bedroom to pack.

Andrea sat quietly amidst the whirlwind of activity, feeling slightly lost. She occupied herself with studying the living room's western decor until she heard the sound of footsteps.

''Who are you?'' came a soft voice.

Andrea looked into the same brown eyes as Kurt's. The hair was also the same shade, but longer, and with curls. The resemblance was so strong, even in a feminine face, that Andrea immediately knew she was seeing Kurt's daughter.

''I'm Andrea, a friend of your father's. He brought me here.''

''Daddy's here?'' The face lit up with a child's delight.

''Yes. Didn't anyone tell you?''

Lynn shook her head, her curls bouncing about her shoulders. ''I just woke up. I had to take a nap with my doll.''

Andrea nodded. ''I always took naps with my doll, too.''

''Wanna see mine?''

''I'd like that. But don't you want to see your father first?''

Lynn cocked her head, listening. "Dad's upstairs. Grandma says I can't go upstairs by myself. I get into trouble."

Andrea smiled at the twinkle in the child's eyes. "Bad trouble?"

"Sometimes." Lynn grinned. "I like to play with Grandma's makeup." She skipped down the hall, her legs moving in perfect coordination. "I'll be right back. My room's downstairs."

When Lynn returned, she was carrying more than a doll. She shyly held out a coloring book and a box of crayons.

"Do you like to color?"

Andrea nodded. "I used to color all the time when I was little."

"Will you color with me?"

"I'd love to." Andrea watched as Lynn sank to the carpet in front of the coffee table, and followed suit. The two of them sat cross-legged while Lynn flipped through her coloring book.

"What page shall we do?" Andrea asked.

Lynn immediately offered her the book. "You pick."

Andrea made her choice. "Here's a nice page. Do you like circus ponies?"

Lynn carefully studied the picture, then nodded. She held out the crayons toward Andrea.

"Thank you, Lynn. I think I'll make my pony brown."

Lynn watched Andrea color for a few minutes before choosing her own crayon. "I'll make mine purple."

Andrea smiled as Lynn proceeded to do just that. "I've never seen a purple pony before."

"Mine is just pretend. Dad says I can use any color I want when it's just pretend."

"That's right, sweetheart. You can."

"Daddy!"

Andrea started, not knowing that Kurt was there, or how long he'd been watching them. Lynn jumped to her feet, scattering crayons as she flew into her father's arms. Their reunion was so touching that Andrea wished she could give them some privacy. She busied herself retrieving the fallen crayons from under the coffee table.

"I hope Lynn hasn't worn your fingers out yet," Kurt said to Andrea. He'd picked up his daughter and perched her on his shoulder, much to Lynn's delight. "She loves to have people color with her."

"She used to color when she was a little girl, Daddy. She told me."

"That's right, I did," Andrea replied. "Shall we finish our pages or would you rather visit with your father?"

"Both!" Lynn squirmed, and he set her back on the floor. She scampered over to sit next to Andrea again. When Lynn was contently coloring purple ponies once more, Andrea spoke to Kurt.

"What with your grandfather and all, I can see I've come at a bad time. If you could call me a cab, I'll get myself a hotel."

"I know it's a lot to ask, but would you mind staying a little longer and watching Lynn?" Kurt asked in a rush of words. "I need to get my parents to the airport if they want to catch the next flight, and Lynn doesn't do well in cars."

"I get sick," Lynn piped up.

"I don't mind staying." Andrea grinned as Lynn started coloring another pony, this one a brilliant shade of green. "I'm glad I can help."

Kurt gave her a grateful smile. "I shouldn't be more than an hour and a half. Lynn, will you be good for Andrea?"

"I won't go upstairs. I won't touch Grandma's things," Lynn promised, not looking up from her page.

"We'll be fine, Kurt. I'll keep a close eye on her. Please tell your parents I hope everything turns out well for your grandfather."

"Thanks, I will. They're out in the car waiting, so I'd better get going. Oh, I'll bring us back some dinner on the way home."

"If you don't have time, I don't mind cooking. Drive safely, Kurt," she added, then turned her attention back to his daughter.

Andrea decided to throw caution to the wind and color another pony a fluorescent orange. She was rewarded by Lynn's approving nod. "Shall I make the tail and mane red?" Andrea asked. "Or purple?"

"Let's ask Daddy."

To her surprise, Andrea saw that Kurt was still watching them, with a strange expression on his face.

"Don't worry, Kurt, I'll take really good care of her," she said, deciding that was why he hadn't left yet.

"I know you will. Be a good girl, sweetheart. Bye, Andrea."

It was almost two hours before Kurt returned. When he did, it was with a bucket of fried chicken and a couple of salads.

"I'm sorry I was so long," he apologized. "Traffic at the airport was a mess, and there was a line at the drive-in."

"That's okay. We were fine," Andrea assured him.

"Look, Dad!" Lynn bounced off the couch with her hands held proudly in the air. "Andrea polished my nails for me. They're pink!"

Kurt studied them with a critical eye. "They look gorgeous," he pronounced.

"I hope you don't mind, but she was so eager to have her nails look like mine," Andrea said. "I can always take the color off before I go."

"I wouldn't worry about it." Kurt tousled his daughter's hair. "Hey, you with the gorgeous nails. How about taking this chicken into the kitchen and setting the table for me? We can use paper plates and plastic forks tonight."

'Can we have sodas instead of milk?''

"We'll have sodas, but you get milk."

"Dad!" Lynn pouted.

"You can have a few sips of mine. Now scoot. Don't forget the napkins."

"I won't."

Kurt waited until Lynn skipped from the room. "Mother said they'll be gone at least a week, maybe more if my grandfather's condition is serious. I sometimes forget he's ninety-one." With a weary motion, Kurt took a seat. "We can't expect him to live forever."

"He might recover," Andrea said hopefully. "I'll keep my fingers crossed."

"We all will." A pause, then, "I'm glad I came home when I did. If nothing else, at least the timing was right. They couldn't have taken Lynn with them."

"A hospital's no place for children," Andrea agreed. "She's absolutely charming, Kurt, and she seems very articulate for her age."

"I'm glad Lynn feels comfortable enough to talk to you. Usually she's very quiet around strangers." He rose from his chair. "Speaking of Lynn, I'd better go see how she's doing. Whenever she's *too* quiet, I worry."

Despite the situation with Kurt's grandfather, dinner was a lively affair. Lynn was in high spirits. She relished her role as hostess, gracing everyone with numerous paper napkins and sunny smiles. Andrea couldn't help responding to her engaging manner.

"Lynn, I really couldn't eat another piece of chicken," she finally said. "I'm full."

"Do you want one?" Lynn held up the cardboard bucket for Kurt. "There's a drumstick and a wing left."

"No, thanks sweetheart. We'll save that for tomorrow. What we should do is get you cleaned up and ready for bed. We had a late dinner."

"But I'm not tired," Lynn protested. "I want to stay up and color."

"No," Kurt said firmly. "You need your sleep."

Lynn pouted, but Kurt was unyielding.

"Let's go. I'll run your bath and help you get undressed."

Lynn pointed at Andrea. "I want her!"

"Andrea's a guest. I'll help you."

"Boys aren't supposed to see girls' underwear. Grandma said so," Lynn said primly.

"Grandma's not here, Lynn. I told you she'll be gone for a while. You'll have to make do with me."

"No." Lynn scowled.

"I don't mind, Kurt, really," Andrea offered. She was rewarded as Lynn slipped a little hand, greasy from fried chicken, into hers. "Lynn can show me where the soap and everything is."

"You do the dishes," Lynn ordered in a commanding voice so like Kurt's that Andrea had to smile.

"She sounds just like you, Kurt," she said with amusement. "Don't worry about us. We'll do fine."

And they did. In no time at all, Lynn was bathed, in a fresh nightgown and in bed.

"I'll get your father to come kiss you good-night."

"I'm right here," Kurt said, stepping into the room. Andrea stood up so he could take her place on the side of the bed. "Did you say your bedtime prayer?" he asked.

"I didn't forget," Lynn said.

"Good girl." Kurt tucked her in. "Now give me a hug and a kiss."

Lynn threw her arms around him and gave him a re-sounding kiss, then whispered something in his ear. Kurt's gaze caught Andrea's. "Lynn wants to know if you'll kiss her good-night."

Andrea felt a flush of pleasure at the request. "Of course I will." She bent over and kissed Lynn on the forehead. Much to her surprise, Lynn sat up and gave her a tight hug. She gently hugged the child back, remaining on the bed until Lynn herself ended the embrace.

"Will you hug my doll, too?" Lynn held up a Raggedy Ann.

Andrea obliged. "Good night, you two."

Kurt turned on the night-light and shut off the overhead one. "Remember, Lynn, Grandpa and Grandma won't be here in the morning, but I will."

"Will you be here, Andrea?"

"I..." Andrea looked from Lynn to Kurt and back again. "I don't know. It's up to your father."

"Can she stay?" Lynn begged.

Andrea and Kurt both watched Lynn hug her doll tight as she waited for an answer. Then Kurt glanced at Andrea, an unfathomable expression on his face.

"Yes, Lynn," he finally said. "She can stay."

CHAPTER ELEVEN

"LYNN'S REALLY ENJOYING your visit," Kurt observed a few days later. They'd put Lynn down for her afternoon nap, and were tidying the living room. Kurt's daughter was a veritable whirlwind when it came to scattering toys.

"And I'm enjoying her, Kurt. She's a lovely child." Andrea was at the coffee table, boxing Lynn's ever-present crayons. "That's one of the few complaints I have with my new job. I don't get a chance to see many children anymore."

"The Grand Canyon isn't exactly a children's park," Kurt replied, his critical eye sweeping the room. "That's about it for the toys. Let's go to the nursery."

Andrea nodded. She'd been at his parents' house since that first night. Things had quickly settled into a easy routine; Andrea tended Lynn while Kurt took care of the meals and the housework. In the mornings they took Lynn for a walk, with a visit to the nearby public playground. In the afternoons while she napped they tidied the house, then worked in Mrs. Marlowe's cactus nursery.

Andrea loved to watch Kurt work with the plants. He was just as capable handling hothouse cactus as he was rafting down the Colorado River. Today, as on the previous days, Andrea ended by pricking herself more often than not, but she didn't care. Every moment spent with Kurt was precious.

"Your hands look like pincushions," Kurt said after they'd been working together a half hour or so. "I told you to wear my mother's gardening gloves."

"I did, but the thorns went right through the leather." Andrea ruefully studied her bleeding fingers. "I guess I still have a lot to learn about the cactus business."

"Why don't you go inside and soak your hands in some antiseptic? I'll finish up here."

Andrea picked up her trowel again. "I'll wait till later."

"Go on," Kurt urged. "I can take care of this myself."

"I know." And Andrea looked up at him with such love, such longing, in her eyes that Kurt's own trowel froze in midair.

"Andrea, don't," he said harshly.

"I can't help it," she whispered.

Then both trowels dropped to the dirt floor as they fell into each other's arms. Kurt's mouth was hard on hers, one hand on her waist, the other threaded tightly through her hair.

In between frenzied kisses Andrea tried to speak, but Kurt refused to let her utter words of love. He covered her mouth again and again until she gave up trying to talk. Only then did he finally put her away from him. They stared at each other in silence. Then Kurt left, and Andrea was left alone, with just the cactus for company.

Kurt rejoined her later, but for the rest of the week the conversation centered on Lynn. Or else they talked about insignificant things—a movie they watched on television, an article Andrea read in the paper. Kurt pointedly refused to discuss anything of a more serious nature. The atmosphere was somewhat tense, but Andrea didn't care. She comforted herself by pretending that she and Kurt were a married couple. The secret pleasure she derived from that fantasy disappeared when she realized their time together was drawing to an end.

Kurt himself was the one who brought that fact home to her three days later.

"Lynn's going to miss you when you're gone," he said. They were once again in the nursery. "She doesn't get a chance to see many new people. I'm glad she's met you."

Andrea swallowed the lump in her throat and played with the sandy soil in a clay pot. "Are your parents on their way home?"

"Yes. I talked to them late last night after you were in bed. My grandfather's much better. In fact, he's being released from the hospital."

"That's good news," Andrea managed to say.

Kurt carefully picked up the last cactus seedling and began to repot it. "Yes, it is."

"What will you do now?"

"Go to work for that environmental protection group. But first I'll have to find a place for myself and Lynn to live. I'd like to be close to her school."

"Have you discussed this with your parents?" Andrea fought to keep calm.

Kurt finished with the last seedling, and started to tidy up his work area. "Not yet, but I will soon. Dad's going to stay on for a while to make sure everything's okay, but my mother should be home in the next couple of days."

A couple of days? Was that all they had left?

"In other words, I'm not needed anymore."

"I didn't say that."

"No, but it's the truth." Andrea put her trowel and gloves away. "So," she asked bluntly, "are we going to keep in touch?"

Kurt didn't have a ready answer, and Andrea sighed.

"It's really kind of ironic, isn't it? Our association began with you wanting to get rid of me. Now it's ending the same way."

"Andrea, that's not true! I'm very grateful for your help with Lynn. But you can't spend the rest of your life here, baby-sitting her. You have a job waiting for you. You've got your own life to live."

"I was hoping to have you in it," she said hoarsely. "*Both* of you."

Kurt left the worktable to stand beside her. He gently grasped her shoulders as he groped for words. "Andrea, I can't say I'm not flattered. I can't even say I'm not tempted. But I don't think I want to start all over again. I risked my heart with Sarah. Once was enough."

"Always, always Sarah!" Andrea cried. "Kurt, you can't spend the rest of your days hiding from life because of one death! I haven't. Dee died only inches away from me, but she'd never want me to stop caring for people because I was hurt by her loss. It would be an insult to what we shared. Life is too valuable! You—*we*—should live it to the fullest. Together."

Andrea held her breath, waiting for Kurt's reaction to her declaration. But his response wasn't what she'd hoped.

He slowly shook his head, and his hands dropped from her shoulders. "I don't have the strength, Andrea. Sarah's death wore me out. There's barely enough left for Lynn."

He took in a deep breath, meeting her gaze. "There's nothing left for you."

Andrea felt something break and shatter deep inside. Time stopped. The face before her blurred.

"Sweetheart, don't look like that," Kurt said urgently. He reached for her hands and held them tight. "I've tried to make it easier for you. I'm leaving the park now instead of in September, as I'd planned."

"Because of Lynn," Andrea said in a dull voice.

"No, I'd planned to work through the summer. It's our busiest time. But you're just getting over Dee. You don't need any more heartaches."

Andrea felt the tears spill. "Why this charade, Kurt? Why pretend it's Dee or Sarah's death that's keeping us apart? Why won't you tell me the truth and say, 'Andrea, I don't want you'?" She swallowed hard. "It would be much kinder."

"Because that would be the biggest lie of all."

Andrea looked up in amazement.

"I *do* want you, Andrea," Kurt said vehemently. He threw out his hands, palms up, in confusion. "I mean, the feeling is there, but the intensity isn't. I live my life once removed—like I'm wrapped up in a thick cocoon. Do you understand?"

Andrea swiped at her cheeks. "No. But whatever's wrong, I still want you."

Kurt shook his head. "Sarah's accident did something to me. I don't know if I'll ever be . . . right . . . again."

Andrea heard the death knell in her heart. Kurt rose to his feet.

"Your coming here hasn't made things easier. The sooner you leave, the better it'll be for both of us."

"Kurt, you've saved so many people! Can't you save yourself?"

Kurt froze at her words, his face a study in pain. "I've tried, Andrea," he said in a hoarse whisper. "Lord knows, I've tried."

Andrea's throat tightened, and for an awful moment she thought life itself had stopped. She finally drew in a deep breath, and when she spoke, she barely recognized the voice coming from her lips as her own.

"Don't ever give up, Kurt."

For both our sakes.

KURT'S MOTHER ARRIVED home the next day. He picked her up from the airport while Andrea stayed with Lynn.

Mrs. Marlowe was happy to report that her father-in-law was recovering nicely. She was even happier to see how well Lynn had done in Andrea's care. But Andrea found it hard to respond to Mrs. Marlowe's praise. All she wanted was to get to the airport and buy a ticket on the earliest shuttle to the Grand Canyon.

Staying in the same house with Kurt had become more than uncomfortable. It was heartbreaking. That was why it was such a jolt when Kurt announced he'd be driving her back.

"Driving me? Kurt, it's a six-hour round-trip! Why don't you just drop me off at the airport?"

"I have to fill out some more paperwork in Jim's office. And I don't want to fly because I have some bulky camping stuff to clear out of my room." He took her suitcase and loaded it into his Jeep.

Andrea hesitated. She wasn't looking forward to spending three hours alone with him in the close confines of a car. What could they say to each other? They'd said it all, except for one thing.

Kurt had never said he loved her. But that was a dream with had no hope, no future.

"Let me drive you back, Andrea. We can turn the radio on if you like," Kurt said quietly, "and dispense with any conversation."

Andrea shifted uncomfortably. She didn't want to seem churlish, but it simply hurt too much to be around him. She was on the point of refusing and calling an airport taxi when Lynn came outside to say goodbye.

"Here," she said, giving Andrea one of her favorite coloring books. "You and Dad can share this at your work."

After that, there was nothing left to do but thank Lynn, hug her goodbye, and get into the Jeep.

True to his word, Kurt switched on Phoenix's classical station. Symphony music flowed through the vehicle, but for once the precise strains of Mozart didn't move her. Andrea's thoughts centered on how lonely her life would be without Kurt. Finally the music became broken and interrupted static. They'd left the flat desert north of Phoenix and were now climbing into the mountains. There was very little traffic on the twisting, turning highway, and the morning remained still. Kurt made several attempts to find another radio station within receiving distance, but gave up after a while.

He tried his CB radio, but found no entertaining air wave chatter available there, either.

"When do you start training with the helicopters?" he asked when the silence in the Jeep became unbearable.

"As soon as I get back, I imagine."

"The scenery's fantastic from a chopper, plus you'll have regular hours. The helicopters can only fly during daylight, so you won't have to worry about working late like the rest of the rangers. You'll enjoy your new job."

"I suppose," Andrea said without much interest. She wasn't looking forward to working without Kurt.

"You don't sound very enthusiastic," Kurt replied with some of his old senior-ranger disapproval.

"I'm just thinking that I'll never get a chance to—to see any of those Indian ruins." *To see you again.*

"We never did get to explore them, did we?"

"No..." Andrea's voice trailed off, and her chest felt painfully tight. This time she was the one who fiddled with the tuning knob, trying to find some music.

Kurt watched her efforts. "We won't pick up anything this far north until around Sedona. Speaking of which, do you want to stop there for anything? A bite to eat or some coffee?"

Andrea turned off the radio and forced herself to respond. "No, thanks. I'm not very hungry. But stop if you

want something." Her polite refusal sounded stiff and un-
natural, as had his offer.

"Maybe you'll change your mind when we get there."

Andrea couldn't stand it. This everyday routine talk of
travel and food was more than she could tolerate. "Kurt..."

"What?"

All of Andrea's love and pain were there for him to see.
Kurt touched her shoulder for just a moment, but it was a
moment that spoke volumes. Andrea, her throat closed,
couldn't continue. She decided she'd be better off saying
nothing. In another few moments she'd start crying like a
baby, embarrassing them both.

At Andrea's silence, Kurt turned his eyes back to the road.

They drove without speaking for a long while as the road
climbed through cactus-covered cliffs and valleys. Occasionally they passed a few slower vehicles, but more often
than not they had the road to themselves.

Andrea pretended an interest in the scenery, while Kurt
concentrated on driving. He pulled into the passing lane to
overtake an old, battered pickup truck.

"Oh, look, aren't they darling?" Andrea said, momentarily distracted from her misery. In the bed of the truck sat
three young bronze-skinned children, their glossy black hair
blowing in the breeze.

"I hate to see kids riding like that. They should be in the
cab, in seat belts."

Andrea continued to study the truck as Kurt's Jeep passed
them. "There's two more children sitting with the driver.
There's no room inside for anyone else."

"Then they should buy a car that'll hold the whole family," Kurt protested.

One of the children saw Andrea, and lifted her hand in a
graceful wave. Andrea smiled and waved back until Kurt's
Jeep left them far behind.

"From the looks of that truck, I don't imagine they have a lot of money to spend."

Kurt gave the truck a last frown of disapproval in his mirror, but nodded, acknowledging the logic of her remark.

They stopped in Sedona after all. Kurt wanted to top up his gas tank, as gasoline prices skyrocketed the closer you got to Grand Canyon Park. Then Andrea changed her mind and decided to have that cup of coffee, which ultimately led to a meal and it was an hour later before they were back on the road.

Andrea expected another silent ride with the Sedona country-western station playing on the radio. She was caught totally unawares when Kurt said, "Do you think you'll ever be down in Phoenix again?"

She fought against the sudden hope. "I haven't thought about it. I don't imagine I'll get much time off from work yet."

"When you do, perhaps you'll consider stopping by and visiting us at our new home. I know Lynn would enjoy your company."

"And you?" she dared to ask.

"And me. But I make no promises, Andrea."

Andrea had to be content with that. The Jeep went on through the mountainous area of northern Arizona. Cactus and desert vegetation mixed first with pines, then with deciduous trees and other vegetation, and finally gave way to them altogether. Traffic was even sparser in this remote area, which was why Andrea noticed the children again.

"There's that old pickup truck we passed a while ago," she said, the first words spoken by either for at least half an hour. "It's up ahead."

Kurt looked far up the road and saw that she was right. "They must have passed us when we stopped to eat."

"I hope the children aren't too cold," Andrea said, worried. "They don't have any jackets. We aren't in the desert anymore."

Kurt frowned. "Let's hope they're wearing good shoes. That old truck can barely climb this stretch of road. If the highway gets any steeper, they'll end up pushing it up the mountain. Or rolling backward."

Andrea felt a superstitious chill go down her spine. "Kurt, don't say that."

Kurt didn't apologize, but he drastically slowed his speed to keep a sedate pace behind the truck. "There aren't any service stations around for miles. I think I'll keep an eye on them for a bit."

Andrea nodded with relief. "At least if they break down, we can give them a ride to the nearest town."

"Pray they don't. It'll be a tight squeeze in here with all those kids."

"Don't forget—" Andrea meant to say "the driver," but she never had the chance.

A noisy *bang* shattered the stillness of the mountain air as one of the truck's worn tires blew with a vengeance. The truck yawed to the left, cut across the opposite lane, then skidded down the steep side of the mountain-road embankment.

The truck rolled onto its side with a sickening crunch of metal. Andrea cried out in horror as she saw the three children in the back thrown out. They flew into the air and bounced off the ground like rag dolls before lying terribly still. The truck rolled away from them, first upside down, then dragging to a stop when it flipped onto its opposite side.

"Kurt, pull over," she implored, but Kurt was already slowing down.

"Get on the CB. Tune in the emergency band on channel nine and get help."

Andrea quickly did, and hung up the microphone just as Kurt parked on the side of the road.

"You triage the three victims outside," he ordered as he leaped out of the Jeep. "I'll check the three inside the truck." He ran around to the back to grab the first aid kit and handed it to her, then they were both hurrying down the embankment.

Andrea found her first victim near the bottom, with the other two children close by and below. Two of the children were conscious and were crying in Spanish for their father.

Andrea didn't know how much English they understood, but she reassured them as best she could. The oldest was covered with serious gashes that would need stitches, possibly even surgery. Andrea stopped the bleeding with compression bandages and tried to calm her.

The second girl's most serious injury appeared to be a broken wrist. Andrea quickly splinted it. She gently told her patient not to move, wishing she spoke Spanish, and wishing even more for the police and ambulance to arrive. She didn't know if the girl understood or not, but as the two sisters were in close proximity, Andrea hoped they'd comfort each other.

She hurried to the third child, a young boy. He was unconscious from a visible head wound, but his pupils were still reactive, a good sign. Andrea treated him for shock, then ran over to the truck.

"What's the situation?" she asked breathlessly.

"The truck is wedged into the rocks," Kurt muttered. "I can't roll it upright, and I can't open this door. It's smashed shut."

"How are the people inside?" Andrea went to the front of the truck and looked in the windshield. There was no movement from the small boy, bigger girl, or the driver.

"The kids are unconscious. So is the father."

"I hate to move them until we get some more help," Andrea said apprehensively. "You saw the way this truck rolled. There could be spinal injuries. We need backboards and cervical collars, not just a motorist's first-aid kid. I say we wait."

"Andrea, I know you're an E.M.T., but trust me, we can't wait."

"We have to! I don't want to paralyze anyone, especially these children, by being too hasty."

Kurt shook his head. "Take in a deep breath. Through your nose."

Andrea did, and her face paled. "I smell gasoline."

"We weren't the only ones who filled up our tank," Kurt said grimly. "It's pouring out of this truck. We don't have any way to put out the flames if it ignites"

"Oh, no." Suddenly she was back in Denver, smelling the jet fuel, then seeing it explode into a fireball. "We can't leave them here, Kurt!" she said frantically.

"We won't. Are the other children far enough away in case this truck goes?"

Andrea nodded, fighting the sick feeling inside her stomach.

"How are they?" Kurt asked as he climbed on top of the vehicle's side.

"The girls have broken bones and lacerations, and one little boy is unconscious from a head wound, but his pupils are reactive."

"That's encouraging." He extended a hand to pull her up.

Andrea scrambled onto the dented, crumpled truck side. "Thank goodness the driver wasn't going very fast. Those children in back could have been a lot worse."

"Let's hope the same applies for these three. We'll have to lift the driver out before we can get to the other two inside. It'll take both of us. He's a big man." Kurt lay down on his stomach and peered in the side window. "At least they all have belts on. I'll hold on to his wrists while you unlatch him. I don't want him falling onto the children.''

"Pray he fits through the window," Andrea said as she took Kurt's former position and stretched down for the seat belt. "Do you have him?"

"Yes."

"Here goes." Andrea pressed the release button, then helped Kurt haul him out of the truck. "Support his neck," she urged as they half carried, half dragged him a safe distance away. Even from this far, Andrea could smell the gasoline.

"He's not bleeding, and he's breathing. That's good enough for the moment," Andrea said after a quick examination. "Let's get the other two out *now*."

They both hurried back to the truck. Just as they climbed back onto the side, the radiator cap blew off with a metal-tearing report. Andrea jumped at the bang and would have fallen from her perch if Kurt hadn't caught her.

"It's only the radiator," Kurt said, trying to calm her nerves, but Andrea brushed his hands away and jumped down through the window of the cab.

"That means the engine's overheated. That means it's still hot. There could be sparks." She practically ripped the seat belt off the boy in the middle of the cab and lifted him up to Kurt. "Take him, and get him the hell away from here! He's not staying in an exploding plane if I can help it."

Kurt froze, and Andrea realized her slip of the tongue.

She quickly corrected herself. "Truck. I mean truck."

"Don't go crazy on me now, Andrea," Kurt ordered tersely. "Are you okay?"

"Yes, I'm fine. *Fine*. Hurry, Kurt," she said with a terrible, overpowering feeling of urgency. "I'll check out this girl while you move the little boy."

Kurt gave her a brief scrutiny, then was gone.

Andrea snorted, trying to rid her nostrils of noxious fumes as she checked the motionless child's vital signs. Satisfied, she unhooked the seat belt. It wasn't really needed to hold her now. The girl was lying on the side, or what was now the bottom, of the truck.

"Come on, sweetheart, let's get you out of here."

Andrea carefully freed the girl's left leg from the crumpled dashboard, then reached for the right. A gentle tug produced no results. Andrea ran her hands down the right leg and ran into mangled metal.

"Oh, no."

She crouched down as far as the limited space and the girl's body would allow and pulled up on the dashboard, but no position allowed her any leverage.

"Damn!" She was still struggling to find a way to free the child's leg when Kurt reappeared.

"What's wrong?" he demanded, his voice hard and driven.

"Her leg is trapped." Andrea gestured toward the maze of crushed metal. "I can't get her out."

Kurt swore. "Maybe the two of us pulling together can. Move over and let me take a look."

Andrea shifted, taking pains to avoid stepping on the unconscious form at her feet.

Kurt slid through the window, and then he was inspecting the dashboard. "She's wedged in pretty tight. Grab hold right here, and let's pull. Watch out for the broken glass. Ready? On three. One, two, three!"

Andrea put her back into it, but their combined efforts were useless.

"Damn! It won't budge."

"We've got to get her out!" Andrea's voice rose as she fought down her panic. "The gas smell is worse. This whole place could blow sky-high!"

"We need tools."

"Tools? Where are we going to get proper rescue equipment? We aren't at work!"

"Andrea, calm down! We'll improvise." Kurt reached underneath the crumpled dash again. "I think we have enough room for the car jack to fit."

"The what?"

"The car jack! We can use it to crank up this dashboard."

"Why didn't I think of that?" Andrea wondered aloud. "Kurt, it just might work. I'll stay with the girl. You go get it."

"No. I want you to go," Kurt ordered. "My Jeep's unlocked. Let me help you out of here."

"Oh, no. I'm not leaving you. *You* go get the car jack. You can run faster than I can. I'm staying with the girl. I have more medical training, remember?"

"Andrea, don't be stupid! This truck could catch fire any minute!"

"*You're* going. I'm staying."

"The hell you are!" Kurt's hands grabbed her by the waist. With one powerful lift, he shoved her up through the window and onto the truck's side. "Now get that jack!"

Andrea couldn't bring herself to leave. "If something happens to you—" She started to shake. Suddenly she understood what Kurt meant about Sarah's death leaving him empty inside. That was what would happen to her if he died. Her eyes were wide with despair and near-panic.

"Move it, Andrea!"

"Kurt, please . . ." she begged.

"You're wasting valuable time! Time we don't have!"

That remark finally got through to her. Andrea immediately vaulted off the upturned side of the truck and starting running up the embankment.

"Your father and brother are okay. We're taking care of your other sister," she called to the children she had tended. "I'll be back to check on you soon."

She was afraid to stop; afraid the truck would explode like her plane had exploded. Afraid Kurt couldn't free the little girl. Afraid he'd become a lifeless, white-sheeted form, a casualty....

Afraid she would lose the man she loved.

Andrea reached the Jeep. She threw her suitcase onto the ground and frantically retrieved the car jack. Then she grabbed the tire iron that went with it. She ran back down the embankment far too fast and tripped. She managed to keep from falling, but dropped the tire iron. It slid down past the dirt and rocks, coming to rest in some bushes.

Andrea forced herself to descend at a safer pace. She dropped to her knees in front of the bushes just as her world exploded.

Even before the racing force of the blast had faded to the sound of burning flames, she knew the truck was gone. And then she screamed.

It was the scream of a victim in pain.

She sank back on her heels, her eyes closed against the horrifying reality. Her grief was so crippling that she couldn't move, couldn't even breathe. She could only feel Kurt's absence, and her own loss.

"Andrea. Andrea, open your eyes, love."

Andrea couldn't believe her ears. She heard her name called again, and felt life start to flow into her anew. Her lungs expanded with one tentative breath, then another.

"Kurt?" Her eyes fluttered open. "Is that you?"

He stood before her with the little girl in his arms. His face was covered with dirt. Pieces of his shirt had been ripped away to reveal bleeding patches of skin, but he was alive. *Alive!*

"In the flesh," he said in a voice as shaky as hers.

"But how..." She struggled to her feet, the car jack still in one hand, the tire iron still in the bushes. "How did you get her out?"

"I kept smelling that gasoline. I was afraid it would ignite. And I was terrified I'd never see you again." A pause. "Finally I just lifted the dashboard myself."

Andrea swayed on her feet, thinking of that twisted metal. "With your bare hands?"

"Yeah."

Andrea dropped the car jack and rushed to check the hands that tenderly cradled the young girl. She stopped when Kurt shook his head.

"I didn't even cut myself." He gave her a tiny grin, a ghost of the real thing, but a grin just the same. "Can you beat that?"

Then Andrea was laughing and crying at the same time, wanting to hug him and then dance with joy... but knowing she couldn't. The children and their father came first.

With Kurt's reappearance, her role as victim ended, and she became a rescuer once more. Side by side they worked together. Finally the police and ambulances arrived, the fire was put out, and the accident victims were loaded onto stretchers.

Kurt's burns were minor. While he was being treated on the scene, Andrea put the car jack, tire iron and her suitcase back in his Jeep. Then one by one, the emergency vehicles started to pull away until there was just a single ambulance left.

"Are you okay?" Andrea asked Kurt. The two of them stood on the side of the road, recovering from their labors and savoring their success.

He smiled, and took her in his arms.

"Kurt, be careful of your burns!" she warned, even as she was nestling closer to him.

"They're nothing, Andrea. Just a few blisters. Really."
He kissed her on the lips—a kiss that held a wealth of emotion—then tucked her under his chin. Andrea was perfectly
content to stand there, feeling his cheek against her hair. She
drank in his sight, his touch, everything about him, still unable to believe the miracle.

"You were right," he murmured. "You were right all
along."

"About what?"

"About not being able to hide forever."

Andrea dreaded seeing the look of pain she knew Kurt's
eyes would hold. But as she lifted her head, her lips parted
in awe. The haunted look was gone. His face was more alive
than she'd ever seen it.

"When you refused to leave the truck, I was terrified you
might be hurt. Afraid you'd turn into another Sarah. So I
threw you out of the truck, and then—"

"And then?" Andrea gently urged, her arms tightening
around his waist.

"And then I realized I've been hiding from death. And in
doing that, I was hiding from life, too."

He turned his face toward the last ambulance, where the
girl who'd been trapped in the truck was finally being lifted
inside. It had taken Andrea and the paramedics longer to
stabilize her than the other victims, but now she could safely
be transported.

They both watched as the ambulance drove away. Then
Kurt turned back to Andrea.

"Life's so precious, and I've wasted so much of it. I could
have been making you happy all this time. Instead I've made
you miserable. I'm a damn fool."

"You are not," Andrea insisted, tears of happiness in her
eyes. "Sarah's death hit you hard. You were hurt. I understand, Kurt. Believe me, I do."

He placed a forefinger under her chin and tenderly tipped back her face. "You were hurt, too. But you didn't hide under a rock. You still took a chance on life. On me."

Andrea gave a shaky laugh. "I never throw in the towel. It must be my flight attendant training."

"No, it's much more than that. I'd like to spend the rest of my life discovering exactly what's in your heart. If you'll let me."

Andrea didn't keep Kurt in suspense. She pulled his face down to hers, and kissed him hard. By the time she was through, he knew exactly how she felt. . . .

CHAPTER TWELVE

"KURT MARLOWE, I CAN'T believe you actually wanted to quit your ranger job," Mrs. Marlowe scolded as she straightened the tie that went with his wedding suit. "As if you'd be happy at some desk job."

"Yes, Mother," Kurt said humbly.

"Don't you 'Yes, Mother' me! Of all the harebrained schemes! You've told me for years that it's better to work within the system for environmental improvement. How can you do that from some office in Phoenix? That's not even near the Canyon, for heaven's sake!"

"You're right, Mom. I wasn't thinking."

Andrea gave Kurt a loving glance and listened with amusement as the dressing-down continued. Now she knew where Kurt had picked up his bossiness.

It was two weeks since the crash. Two weeks since Kurt had finally laid Sarah to rest and literally become a new man. He'd reinstated himself at his old job, and he'd asked Andrea to marry him. That had been right after the rescue.

Andrea remembered his words.

"I still have to take care of Lynn, Andrea. I've been a weekend father for far too long."

She and Kurt were in each other's arms, still clothed, on the bed of a Sedona hotel. They'd needed to file an eyewitness police report regarding the accident. After that, Andrea had suggested staying in town. She was physically tired, but Kurt was in worse shape. In addition to his injuries, he was emotionally drained. Andrea didn't want him back on the road. They would wait to hear from the hospital on the condition of the family.

"As much as I love you—" Kurt's face had taken on a soft glow "—I need to make plans for my daughter. I can't shirk my obligations."

"So you do love me." Andrea sighed blissfully. "I've waited forever to hear that."

Kurt pulled her onto his chest and gave her a long, satisfying kiss. "I've waited a long time to say it. But because of what happened to Sarah, I didn't think I had the courage to love again."

"And now you do?" Andrea asked, needing to hear the answer once and for all.

"Yes."

Andrea gave a big sigh of happiness, and Kurt tenderly kissed her again and again.

"With one part of myself, of my heart, I'll always love Sarah. And that same part will always mourn her, especially for Lynn's sake. But life goes on. I don't want to live in the past anymore. I want a future with you."

"And with Lynn," Andrea added, running her fingers lovingly through his hair. "I want to be a real mother to her. I think she's young enough to accept me. We made a good start the week I stayed at your parents'."

Kurt had lifted his eyes to hers in wonder. "You really mean that?"

"Yes, of course. I've always liked children, and I'll love Lynn even more because she's yours."

That much was true. First Kurt and now Lynn had found a place in her heart. She had room for them both.

"With my job on the helicopters, I'll have regular hours. I'll be quite able to take care of Lynn when she gets home from school. We'll be a real family, the three of us."

And maybe later, even more . . .

Kurt's eyes had glowed at her words, and then he shook his head. "Don't tempt me, Andrea. I can always take that environmental job in Flagstaff instead of Phoenix. That way I'd be home for Lynn," he said. "I don't expect you to make such a sacrifice."

"What sacrifice? Don't be silly. I love Lynn already, and I love *you*." She kissed him on the forehead to emphasize her words. "You'd be miserable at a desk job. If you feel so strongly about being home for Lynn, why not just switch to flying rescue helicopters after we all move to Flagstaff?"

"Full-time?"

"Why not? It's your job as an instructor and floater that gives you such long hours. As a rescue pilot, you'd be home at sunset."

"And I'd make sure I have a certain E.M.T. as my crew," Kurt promised. "Rank does have its privileges."

"Kurt, you know I'd love to keep working with you. But that's not the point. I think you should stay with the park service. You should keep helping people. That's what you do best." Andrea shivered, remembering. "I couldn't have saved that girl in the truck. I would never have thought to use the car jack to free her."

"Yes, you would," he contradicted.

Andrea had smiled at his loyalty. "Well, maybe, but I wouldn't have thought of it fast enough. I certainly couldn't have strong-armed her free. That whole family wouldn't be together today if it wasn't for you."

Andrea thought about the phone call they'd eventually received at the hotel. The hospital said the girl's leg injuries weren't irreversible. Miraculously, everyone would eventually recover with no ill effects.

"That girl in the truck could easily have been a Lynn or an Emily. I know your environmental work is important, Kurt, but so is what you do now."

"I'll never give up working for the protection of the Canyon," Kurt had said slowly. "You need to know that if I stay with the park service, I'll still work to change the Grand Canyon's environmental practices. Other major parks like Yosemite limit visitors on a regular basis. I think we should do the same."

"That might take years," Andrea had said with satisfaction. "So I don't want to hear any more talk about quitting in the near future."

She recalled how Kurt bent his elbow and propped his head over hers. His gaze was loving as he said, "Between you and Jim and my mother, I don't know who's worse."

Andrea smiled. "With the three of us, you never had a chance at resigning."

"Are you at least going to let me propose properly, or have you arranged that, too?"

"Kurt, don't tease," Andrea said with embarrassment before she saw the twinkle in his eyes.

Kurt gently played with a strand of her hair. "Actually, now that I think about it, your arrangements aren't that bad. You were the one who requested a single room for two. You'll probably seduce me, then demand I make an honest woman out of you in the morning. Which I'd agree to in an instant, by the way," he added. "Are you game?"

Andrea felt her heart skip a beat. Kurt was actually in high spirits. For the first time she saw Kurt as he was meant to be—not weighed down by an old tragedy. The perpetually coiled tension about him was gone. He was relaxed and happier than she'd ever seen before.

"Game for what?" she replied in kind, fighting back the tears of joy. "Seducing you or marrying you?"

Kurt laughed, a rare, precious sound. Andrea knew she would treasure this moment the rest of her life.

"Both, my love, both."

As his lips claimed her mouth, Andrea finally realized that everything was going to be all right....

Now she stood in her wedding gown, watching Mrs. Marlowe scold her son. Finally his tie was straightened to her satisfaction, completing the somber, formal tuxedo that couldn't begin to disguise his joy.

"It's bad enough that you're staying at a bunch of old ruins on your honeymoon. Everyone I know goes to Hawaii or Niagara Falls," Mrs. Marlowe lamented.

"There's only one Niagara Falls, Mother, and Hawaii just has seven islands. Arizona, on the other hand, has thousands of archeological sites. I wanted to make sure Andrea wouldn't be bored."

The light of passion that flared in his eyes as he looked Andrea's way told everyone she would have no complaints about boredom. Andrea blushed, but her eyes eagerly met his. An embarrassed Mrs. Marlowe cleared her throat.

"Umm, yes, I see. But why you couldn't get married in a church instead of outside is beyond me," she continued to chide, even as Kurt pulled away from his mother's fussing and took Andrea in his arms. "How you convinced Andrea's parents here to go along with this crazy scheme of yours I'll never know."

"We do have a minister, Mother," Kurt said, his whole attention focused on his bride.

Andrea thrilled to his touch as his fingers adjusted the veil the breeze was tugging astray. Her long white gown swished around her ankles in the gentle wind.

"What's more, we have this."

Kurt gestured behind him toward the Grand Canyon, which formed the backdrop to their wedding party. The cloudless sky was a brilliant azure blue. The sun shone off the rainbow of colors with a special radiance Andrea knew was just for them.

"You can't convince me any man-made church is more fitting."

Mrs. Marlowe took in the majesty below her, but it was clearly her son's happiness that caused her to relent. "No, I suppose not. Come on, Lynn, it's time to take our places."

Lynn shyly stepped next to Emily, for Andrea had insisted on having both as her wedding attendants. She saw Kurt smile when the two little girls joined hands.

You have to live in the present, and look toward the future, Andrea thought. And how very glad she was that she and Kurt had done just that. *I'm so happy. Wherever you are, Dee, I hope you're happy, too.*

Then, like Kurt, Andrea put her thoughts of the past away, until only her love for him filled her heart.

The minister motioned them to approach.

"Wait a minute," Andrea said suddenly. "Where's Jim?"

"Here I am!" Jim yelled out.

"What in the world?" Mrs. Marlowe exclaimed, her hands flying to her cheeks.

Jim was leading a small burro with a wreath of fresh carnations around its neck. "It's your wedding present, of course. It isn't often that my toughest senior ranger goes soft over a baby burro. Well, here she is, Kurt, weaned and cured, just like you wanted." He handed Kurt the lead. "She's all yours."

Andrea turned toward her husband-to-be in amazement. He wore a sheepish expression as he protested, "I'm not going soft!" Before she could say a word, he added, "I just felt Lynn ought to learn to ride before her first Canyon mule ride. That's all."

"Then for Lynn's sake, I thank you." Andrea gave him a kiss on the cheek.

"Hey, you're supposed to be thanking *me!*" Jim said, laughing.

"Forget it, Jim," Kurt replied, his eyes only on Andrea until his daughter tugged at the tail of his tuxedo.

"Is she really mine, Dad?" Lynn asked excitedly. "Do we get to keep her?"

Emily immediately joined in. "I want a burro, too," she begged her parents. "Please, Mom, Lynn gets to have one!"

"Now look what you've started, son," Mrs. Marlowe moaned.

"Do I get to name her?" Lynn asked.

The baby burro looked up, as if realizing she was the topic of conversation. She turned her head and placidly began to eat a carnation.

Andrea smiled as Kurt immediately intervened. Trust the man she loved to keep things under control.

"You're not supposed to eat those." Kurt gently pulled the rest of the flower from burro's mouth.

"I want a burro at *my* wedding," Emily piped up, much to the amusement of all except Mrs. Marlowe.

"Burros do *not* belong at weddings," she stated firmly.

"I disagree." Andrea stepped next to Kurt, one hand on his arm, the other gently stroking the animal's soft nose. "I'm glad to see her again—it reminds me how much has changed since the day we rescued her." She smiled into Kurt's eyes, a smile meant just for him. "Yes, I'd definitely say she belongs at our wedding."

Kurt's mother looked from Andrea to Kurt, shook her head in amused resignation, and was silent.

"Take her lead, Jim," Kurt ordered. "Girls, you stay back from the burro, at least until the ceremony's over." He passed the rope to Jim, then immediately cupped Andrea's face.

"Are we ready now, love?"

"Oh, yes." Andrea beamed with joy. "I've been ready a long, long time. But I'm so happy, I don't mind waiting."

"Well, I do." Kurt placed his arm around her waist. The singing colors of the Canyon framed her white bridal dress, while the silver reflection of the Colorado danced far below.

"I love you, Andrea Claybourne."

Andrea's heart overflowed with happiness, and her gaze conveyed what her lips could not. The minister opened his book and cleared his throat. Family and friends gathered closer. Lynn's small fingers slipped into Andrea's left hand, and Kurt's strong, capable hand clasped her right.

Andrea gave them all a brilliant smile, then she leaned her head against Kurt's shoulder.

"Dearly beloved . . ."

Where do you find hot Texas nights, smooth Texas charm and dangerously sexy cowboys?

COWBOYS AND CABERNET

Raise a glass—Texas style!

Tyler McKinney is out to prove a Texas ranch is the perfect place for a vineyard. Vintner Ruth Holden thinks Tyler is too stubborn, too impatient, too... Texas. And far too difficult to resist!

CRYSTAL CREEK reverberates with the exciting rhythm of Texas. Each story features the rugged individuals who live and love in the Lone Star State. And each one ends with the same invitation...

Y'ALL COME BACK...REAL SOON!

Don't miss *COWBOYS AND CABERNET* by Margot Dalton. Available in April wherever Harlequin books are sold.

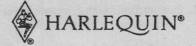
HARLEQUIN®

THE TAGGARTS OF TEXAS!

Harlequin's Ruth Jean Dale brings you
THE TAGGARTS OF TEXAS!

Those Taggart men—strong, sexy and hard to resist...

You've met Jesse James Taggart in FIREWORKS!
Harlequin Romance #3205 (July 1992)

And Trey Smith—he's THE RED-BLOODED YANKEE!
Harlequin Temptation #413 (October 1992)

And the unforgettable Daniel Boone Taggart in SHOWDOWN!
Harlequin Romance #3242 (January 1993)

Now meet Boone Smith and the Taggarts who started it all—
in LEGEND!
Harlequin Historical #168 (April 1993)

Read all the Taggart romances!
Meet all the Taggart men!

Available wherever Harlequin Books are sold.